VIKING BEAST

VIKING WARRIORS VOLUME 3

EMMANUELLE DE MAUPASSANT

DARK CASTLE
PRESS

First published in 2019

CONTENTS

VIKING

BEAST

EMMANUELLE
DE MAUPASSANT

NOTES FROM THE AUTHOR

Welcome to my 'Viking Warriors' steamy romance series.

Svolvaen and Skálavík are fictitious, as are my characters.
While the superstitions and rituals related in this series are based on
true Norse beliefs, I've taken liberties in shaping them. You'll
recognize the Norse myths, though with many omissions and told
with my own emphasis.

I've described the longhouse much as we believe it would have
appeared, with deep benches along each interior wall (used for sitting
and sleeping). A central firepit provided warmth and a means of
cooking, with smoke drawn through a hole in the roof.

While it's commonly believed that most longhouses were
'windowless', the sagas of *Brennu-Njáls* and *Grettis* both mention
openings akin to windows (without glass but using skins which could
be drawn back).
I used this device most prominently in Viking Wolf, as it served my
plot.

Happy Reading
Em

CAST

Brought from Northumbria
Elswyth - our heroine
Faline - Elswyth's stepdaughter

Svolvaen residents
Gunnolf ('fighting wolf') – Eirik's older brother
Asta - Gunnolf's wife
Eirik ('eternal ruler') – brother to Gunnolf
Helka – sister to Eirik and Gunnolf
Guðrún and **Sylvi** – Gunnolf's thralls (slaves who undertake household duties)
Astrid – a village woman who befriends Elswyth
Ylva - Astrid's daughter
Torhilde – Astrid's neighbour
Bodil – a former lover of Eirik
Anders – the blacksmith
Halbert – the blacksmith's son
Olaf – friend to Eirik

❖

Svolvaen residents (deceased)
Hallgerd – the previous jarl (uncle to Eirik, Helka and Gunnolf)
Wyborn ('war bear') - father to Eirik, Helka and Gunnolf
Wybornsson
Agnetha - sister to Hallgerd, married Wyborn
Vigrid – Helka's first husband

❖

Bjorgyn residents
Jarl Ósvífur
Leif Ósvífursson – oldest son of Jarl Ósvífur
Freydís Ósvífursdóttir – sister to Leif

❖

Skálavík residents
Jarl Eldberg (the Beast)
Sigrid - old Jarl Beornwold's sister
Sweyn, Thoryn, Fiske, Hakon, Ivar, Rangvald (Eldberg's sworn-men)
Ragerta and **Thirka** - Eldberg's house thralls

❖

Skálavík residents (deceased)
Bretta - Eldberg's wife
Beornwold (Bretta's father - the former jarl)

GLOSSARY

to go 'a-viking' – to go raiding/marauding
Alfablót – the festival of the dead
blót – ritual sacrifice
dagmal – morning meal
Dökkalfar – the spirits of the dark
draug – the returning dead, restless due to some injury suffered in life
jarl – the chieftain of the community
Jörmungandr – the serpent which encircles the Earth and, on releasing
its tail, will begin the events of *Ragnarök*
Jul – the New Year festival
Lithasblot – the harvest festival
nattmal – late afternoon/early evening meal
Ostara – the spring festival
skald – a travelling storyteller/bard
thrall – a slave (often captured during raids)
Valknut – Odin's symbol—three interlocking triangles with the power
of life over death

1

ELDBERG

May, 960AD

He woke to the crackle of flames. Sparking and spitting, the roof was alight, glowing dull through a veil of acrid smoke.

He sat up to kick at the furs, to draw breath to shout, but his throat closed against the foul ash.

He shook his sleeping bride, but she made no answer.

By the gods! They had to get out.

With eyes smarting, he lifted her from the bed.

The blaze was moving quickly, the flames licking through the timbers.

Eldberg buried his face in Bretta's shoulder. Her head was flung back.

Find the door.

He managed several steps, though his bare feet were scorched. Nothing mattered but for them to escape. He was almost there when something struck his head.

He called her name as he fell; or thought he did.

And then, though the room was bright with flames, there was only darkness.

2

ELDBERG

Eldberg lay three days and nights, his body not yet ready to wake. When he did, it was to searing pain.

The memory of that night returned with the force of all Thor's thunder, striking fear in Eldberg's heart. Already he knew his fate, but would not accept it, not until the truth had been spoken aloud.

Sweyn, the commander of his battle-guard, stood to one side, his face severe. Behind him was Fiske, Rangvald, Hakon, Ivar. None would meet his gaze—not even Thoryn, the most steadfast of his sworn men.

Only Sigrid—Bretta's aunt—summoned the courage. "The great hall's roof lies smouldering." Her voice rose not above a whisper. "Ivar and Thoryn battled through the flames to drag you out."

Sigrid drew a deep breath. "Thrice, Thoryn returned for Bretta, but the smoke was too thick, the heat too ferocious." She bit her lip. "Rangvald and Fiske held him back from trying again. My Bretta! She is...gone, my Jarl."

A shudder passed through him, of sudden, terrible despair. He lay still, willing command of his desire to howl in anguish. His wife! The woman he'd wed at her father's behest—a contracted marriage to tie his loyalty to Skálavík. The wife for whom he'd never expected to feel love. The wife who had adored him—inexplicably, and without reservation.

And the child.

His hands bunched the cloth upon which he lay.

His child. Six months in the womb.

Eldberg swallowed back sour bile and set his jaw. With renewed intensity, he scanned the faces before him. Motioning Sigrid away, he looked to Thoryn.

The man's misery was etched deep, his lips parched and white. Thoryn was brave and loyal; he would have given his life to save Bretta.

Eldberg turned to Sweyn. Of all his men, he was most like himself —ambitious and unforgiving, able to act without remorse or mercy.

Stolen as a child by marauding berserkers, Eldberg had been enslaved until his fifteenth year, when his height and strength and his relentless will had earned him a true place among them. He'd known only their ways—where brutality and savagery were rewarded.

As Beornwold's mercenary, paid to join his raiding trips to the West, Eldberg had fought alongside Sweyn these fifteen years, and had seen his jealousy—for Eldberg was soon favored above all others. The old jarl had chosen him to marry Bretta, to sire Beornwold's line, and to take his mantle.

Sweyn obeyed through no sense of brotherhood, but because it brought him command over others—in his jarl's name.

Keep your enemies close, Beornwold had told him long ago.

Eldberg frowned. He'd heeded those words well, allowing Sweyn authority, satisfying the need that drove the other man, making use of it. Had Sweyn become greedy? Had he wished his jarl's death and that of his heir—yet to be born?

The Norns had unpicked only one strand of that thread upon their loom.

The conviction assailed him; Sweyn had planned everything. He'd sought to kill him and take his place. He'd murdered Bretta!

"How did the fire start?" Eldberg kept his voice level, addressing Sweyn alone. Despite his fury, he would seek evidence carefully.

"That I have learnt, my Jarl, and have the culprit shackled." He gestured, sending Ivar and Fiske from the room. "We captured him on the very night of his crime. A spy from Svolvaen, sent to murder you."

Summoning his strength, Eldberg raised himself a little. "Lift me, Sweyn."

His commander took him beneath the arms, hauling him to a seated position. Through his left side, swathed in salve and linens, came a jolt of pain greater than Eldberg had anticipated. But he'd endured many wounds; this was no different.

Sigrid darted forward to place pillows behind his back. Eldberg nodded curtly, acknowledging her care. She, at least, he could trust. Sigrid had raised Bretta as her own and respected the love between her niece and jarl.

The man dragged into the room, hunched over, was a head shorter than those around him. Fiske and Ivar supported him on either side, for he was unable to stand. His head and limbs hung limp, his wrists and ankles bent at unnatural angles. Both eyes were puffed closed within his bloodied face. His jaw hung slack—broken.

"The man has been beaten near to death." Eldberg fixed Sweyn with an icy stare.

"I interrogated him. It was necessary."

Eldberg narrowed his gaze. "And now he can no longer speak."

"I discovered all you need to know, my Jarl. Hallgerd's successor, Gunnolf of Svolvaen, sent him. From a fishing boat he swam into the northern cove and climbed the cliffs hand over hand. Waiting until darkness, he entered the woodlands, watching several days before he acted."

"Undetected? All that time?"

Sweyn shrugged. "He is more weasel than warrior, adept at hiding."

"And why? What of the treaty? Nigh thirty summers have passed. Why should this Gunnolf act so foolishly? Svolvaen is no match for our strength."

"You answer your own question, Jarl." Sweyn dipped his head. "In fear of what we once were, and what we have the power to be,

Gunnolf sent his man to collect what information might be useful." He glanced up again. "And to wound us most mortally, by causing your death."

Eldberg shifted, wincing. "Pull back his head. I would see him."

Sweyn grasped the man's hair at the crown.

In the heat of battle, Eldberg thought nothing of severing a man's limb or head, but the state of the prisoner made him grimace. Being unable to close his mouth, bloodied drool hung from his chin. His cheek and nose were likely broken, the flesh bruised and raw.

Eldberg liked to look a man in the eyes, but the swollen flesh prevented him from doing so. He returned his gaze to Sweyn, whose own granite-grey eyes remained impassive.

"How was it done?"

Sweyn gave answer without hesitation. "He learnt of your chamber's position within the longhouse. He carried a bow and was able to fire flaming arrows to where they would have most effect. By the time our watchmen saw the flames, your chamber was already imperiled."

Eldberg was assailed, most suddenly, with the memory of Beornwold's funeral. Sweyn had soaked a strip of linen in fish oil and wrapped it close behind the arrow head. This he'd dipped into the fire cauldron before setting aim for the pyre upon the old jarl's longship. Sweyn was not only adept with sword and axe but one of their most masterful archers.

Eldberg stared meaningfully at Sweyn. "The cur was well-prepared. Were he able to answer me, I would ask him much."

If his sworn-man related the truth, the assassin before them had been cunning and courageous, and favored by the gods—for the guards under Sweyn's command swept the perimeter of Skálavík daily.

The town's trade in metals and weapons, made from the ore dug from the mountains, had made Skálavík wealthy. There was hardly need for raiding to bring bounty to their coffers. Many from across the region came to them. Their warriors were engaged now in protecting the town's commerce, ensuring its security.

"What now, my Jarl?" Sweyn wet his lips. "A few blows of my axe and we may toss him by parts to the pigs."

A gurgle rose from the prisoner's throat, and his feet scrabbled momentarily before he hung limp again.

"'Tis fitting," Eldberg declared. "If a man is willing to inflict pain, he must expect like for like." He held his commander's gaze, but Sweyn did not flinch.

Signaling his wish to lie down again drew Rangvald and Hakon forward. Eldberg blanched as they aided him but did not voice his discomfort. The burns would take time to heal, but they were nothing compared to the wounds that tore his heart. The grief would become part of him. He would focus on that pain—would feel it and remember.

And a day of reckoning would come.

He closed his eyes, leaning back. "Hold the wretch's head in the fire pit, and keep it there until I no longer hear his screams."

At last he slept.

In his dream, he clasped her close. Her skin was soft and her hands caressing, though her fingers were chilled.

Don't leave. I need you. Stay with me, Bretta!

But his arms could not hold her.

Waking, he was soaked in sweat, alone, and his chest so tight he could hardly breathe. She was gone forever—his only love. His wife, and the child she carried—his son or daughter.

He wanted to howl to Odin and Thor, to swear vengeance by all the gods for what had been taken from him. Casting back his head, he gave a mournful cry. Let others hear and quake to know his anguish. He would find no rest until he'd devoured his enemies. Let them know the beast he was and fear him—a man disfigured not just in body but in soul: The Beast of Skálavík.

3

ELSWYTH

July 30th, 960AD

The fjord was filled with shimmering light and the squawk of gannet chicks.

Eirik pulled deep on the oars, the warmth of gold-veined summer on his bare back. His shoulders flexed as he rowed—bronzed and lean-muscled. The waves lapped softly. Letting the boat glide, he lifted the oars from their cups, safely stowing them. He made a show of placing his hands behind his head and resting his gaze where I'd hitched up my gown of green linen to enjoy the sun on my skin.

"I prefer you naked, wife."

"Not wife, yet." I suppressed a smile. "I'm free to do as I please until the vows are spoken."

"You wish to disobey me?" Eirik's eyes flickered with mischief. "If it's punishment you desire, raise your skirts and I'll gladly redden your backside."

"And what of you, husband?" I pulled my dress higher and opened my legs, offering him the view he sought. "Will I need to punish you? Or will you forsake your wickedness once we're wed?"

In a single movement, he knelt before me. "I have eyes only for you, wife." He winked, making clear where he directed his admiration.

I tugged back his head. "Helka's been teaching me how to use the bow. Give me cause, and you'll need to guard your own behind."

He pretended to ponder, and I jerked harder, laughing.

His hands came to rest just above my knees. His palms were calloused from wielding not just sword and axe but hoe and spade, from farming in the fields, but they were warm, and his touch gentle.

"You need not doubt my fidelity." He sealed his promise with a kiss upon my inner thigh. "There will be only happiness." He continued upward, his golden beard grazing soft against my skin. "And many children."

His voice was husky as he brought his mouth to my curls. His tongue found me, the tip flicking back and forth. I moaned, feeling my wetness grow. The familiar ache stirred low in my belly. Eirik had shown me what it was to be desired and to crave in return.

His heart was mine, he said. Yet, I held back some part of me—afraid of him seeing how much I needed him.

Not so very long ago, he'd left Svolvaen at Gunnolf's command, to make a marriage of alliance. Duty was stronger than love, he'd told me. Even now, on the eve of our wedding, I didn't know if I could trust my heart to his care.

Nor did I know if I could trust myself.

In Eirik's absence, I'd believed myself betrayed—that Eirik had never loved me, that he'd come back wedded. Piece by piece I'd died, letting Gunnolf claim what Eirik had so carelessly cast away, until I barely remembered who I was. I hadn't wanted to remember. It had been a time of strange, consuming oblivion.

I pushed against Eirik's shoulders, suddenly unsure of myself, but he grasped my waist and pulled me firm toward his mouth.

"I want you." He buried his tongue deeper, reaching where his cock would soon follow. "And this—forever."

I struggled only briefly, holding fast to the raised portion of the deck until I could think only that he must not stop. It had always been so, from the first days, when he'd come to Holtholm as a raider, and I'd been powerless to deny him.

I slid my fingers through his hair, yielding to the urgent hunger of his mouth. With yearning pain, I wanted him, but he took his time, for it aroused him to see me so. He teased me long and slow, until my belly tightened, and I shuddered.

Unfastening the brooches that held my gown, he pulled away all that I wore, until I lay as naked as he, and he moved to cover me. He pressed his lips to my eyelids and my forehead, and to the hollow of my throat, scooped back my hair to nuzzle behind my ear.

I twined my arms about his neck, welcoming his weight and the sliding push of his penetration.

"So tight. So warm." He buried his face against my breast, suckling with each thrust, yielding sharp pleasure.

Caressing his buttocks, I pulled him deeper, wrapping my legs around his.

"Eirik!" I breathed his name as a searing jolt seized me. I raised my hips to receive him, crying at the depth of his final invasion.

I listened to the slap of water against the side of the boat as we lay together.

Eirik cradled me. "You're mine, Elswyth." Tenderly, he stroked my hair. "I wish only…"

I raised myself to my elbow, wishing to know what troubled him, but he shook his head.

"'Tis foolish— for she is dead these thirty years."

Sitting up, I placed my hand over his heart. He'd spoken of his mother only once—of her abduction when Eirik had been but three summers old.

"Do you wish to tell me of it?"

A shadow crossed his face. "It changes nothing to dwell on the past."

I brushed the hair from his eyes. "But it may ease your heart and—"

He caught my wrist and turned my palm to meet his lips, holding it there for several moments. "You wish to know what pains me, wife, that you may share in understanding."

"I do."

Eirik returned my hand to his chest, holding it there with his own. He breathed slowly, gathering his thoughts.

"For many years, I had no knowledge. Only later did I discover what no one wished to tell me. My grandfather, jarl in his time, married Ingrid of Skálavík and two children were born: first Hallgerd, then my mother Agnetha. When Agnetha reached the age of betrothal, they promised her to Beornwold, Ingrid's nephew—Jarl of Skálavík."

I bit my lip, for I knew that such a contract had never been fulfilled.

"Hallgerd became jarl on his father's death and spurned the contract, giving Agnetha to his closest friend, Wyborn."

"A love-match?"

Eirik nodded. "Half of the dowry that would have come with Agnetha was sent to Beornwold in recompense, and it seemed the matter was settled. My mother soon bore Gunnolf, followed by Helka, and myself. More than six years passed."

I frowned, knowing that blood feuds began over far lesser offences. "But Beornwold had not forgotten."

"No, Beornwold neither forgot nor forgave. After my grandmother's death, he came to take Agnetha by force, saying that what he'd been promised should not be withheld.

"And Hallgerd beat the Skálavík raiders into retreat."

"Aye," said Eirik, "but not before my father fell, and my mother was taken by Beornwold." He squeezed my hand. "Svolvaen emptied its stores and coffers for her release, and a pact was signed. The boat maker and his two oldest sons went to Skálavík to build three dragonships. In return, there was to be no further conflict."

I swallowed, wondering if I was brave enough to ask more. "And did she speak of what passed during her captivity?"

Eirik made no reply, merely looking out over the fjord. At last, he said, "When Svolvaen sent a ransom for her release, Beornwold sent her back, but she wasn't the same. I woke up one morning and she was gone again. Everyone was searching. It was the next day that a fishing boat found her floating, out here."

"Oh, Eirik!"

His mother had taken her life, grieving for the husband lost to her, and for the lost part of herself taken by Beornwold. The saddest part was that Eirik, Helka, and Gunnolf had lost them both.

Eirik gathered up my under tunic, passing it over my head, then held out my green gown, helping me into it before pulling on his own clothes. "My brother grew up thinking Hallgerd weak for having signed the truce. He always spoke of revenge for our parents' deaths but knew we lacked Skálavík's strength. An attack would have brought the end of everything."

"And what do you wish, Eirik?"

"I, too, have hungered for justice, but I won't ask others to lay down their lives to appease my sorrow. We all live with wounds from our past. It's wisest to find a way to see beyond them." Moving to the other end of the boat, he fitted the oars once more.

"We'll complete the fortifications begun by Gunnolf once the summer's crop is harvested, but I intend no feud with Skálavík. Beornwold is dead these four seasons past, and the bad blood has ended."

We said no more as Eirik turned the vessel about. The sky had grown dusky—a soft twilight before the brief hours of darkness.

My heart should have been filled with joy, but a secret lodged there, held close these weeks past. I hadn't been sure at first, but my conviction had been growing, and I needed to tell Eirik. He would soon notice himself, and I must speak before that time came.

For so long I'd desired a child, and Freya had answered me, but my past clung upon my shoulders.

Gunnolf had died on the night Eirik had returned to Svolvaen, yet I remained in his power, for I feared the babe I carried had not been sired by the man I loved.

19

Just another few weeks, and I will tell him.

But tell him what?

That his own brother, having made me his bed thrall, planted his seed where Eirik failed? That his heir might be born of that lust, rather than the love between us?

Eirik had sworn forgiveness of all that had passed in those precarious days—but would he forgive this? Wasn't it better for me to pretend certainty and claim the conceiving to have occurred only after Eirik's return? It might even be true.

I'd wanted a marriage built upon trust and honesty. Instead, it would begin with a lie.

4

ELSWYTH

July 31st, 960AD

"A toast to our jarl and his good lady," bellowed Olaf from where he stood upon the table. "May the gods give us all such wives —clever and resourceful, and with beauty exceeded only by Freya."

Eirik grinned, and there was much banging of cups.

"You should go looking in the forest to find your sweetheart, Olaf!" Anders hollered from the other side of the hall. "Some bear is sure to be willing to embrace you."

"No need to go so far," guffawed Halbert. "The sheep pen is right outside. Half a dozen darlings to choose from there, Olaf!"

The others roared in laughter, men and women alike, making ribald gestures. Guðrún, walking amongst them with her jug of mead, was tossed from one lap to the next, until she landed upon Olaf's—to much cheering and her own blushes, for all knew she nursed tender feelings for him.

I couldn't help but feel content. Since my arrival in Svolvaen, I'd fought for acceptance and approval. Now, seeing how I made Eirik happy, his people had granted me their blessing.

Only Bodil, standing apart, scowled as I glanced her way.

You can keep your sour looks, for I'm married now, and Eirik will have no more of you! I gave her an innocent smile, but she continued to glower, and I reprimanded myself for pettiness. Though she'd once been Eirik's lover, he'd shown no inclination for her since bringing me to Svolvaen.

I resolved to enjoy the merriment, which had moved to the bracing of elbows for arm wrestling. With so much mead drunk, the bouts quickly escalated, until there were several men tumbling on the floor, red in the face. The losers of each bout received a light punish-ment—a horn of ale brought for drinking in one long draught, to more cheers.

I'd lived in Svolvaen a full year, but I was yet to grow accustomed to the boisterous nature of such gatherings. With some relief, I retreated—it being a bride's privilege—asking Sylvi to set aside the platter she carried and come with me to comb my hair. I'd worn it loose today as Eirik liked best, falling to my waist.

From beyond the wooden partition of Eirik's chamber, there came the sound of stamping feet and shouts of encouragement as the men's games continued. I closed my eyes as Sylvi drew the carved bone through my hair.

She spoke softly as she worked. "May the gods send you their blessings, and all the happiness a bride may wish for."

I touched her hand in gratitude. "You've always been kind, Sylvi—a good friend."

She squeezed my fingers in return, then drew the comb again. She gathered back my hair from my shoulders, being careful not to dislodge the copper brooches clipped to the looped straps of my gown. Sylvi had dyed the wool herself, steeping it in the bark of mountain alder, and the color had sprung vivid. I tilted my head back and absentmindedly fingered the adornment on my bodice. Not just any brooch, but the ivory Asta had gifted to me before her death.

Asta.

I could still see her face so clearly.

Since the night of Gunnolf and Faline having fallen into the chasm upon the cliffs, the rumors of Asta's spirit walking had ceased. I was glad, for that other realm had no place in this.

Gunnolf's body had washed ashore after some days, though Faline's had never been found. With his sword and shield upon his chest, we'd sent the jarl to the next life upon the pyre of a burning ship.

I wondered if he and Asta had found the peace that had eluded them in this world. There had been too much death and too much unhappiness, but Eirik was right—we would begin anew.

We'd spoken our vows that morning, upon the shore of the fjord, alongside Helka and Leif, with all Svolvaen bearing witness to our marriages.

Helka would soon return to Bjorgyn with her new husband, there to enjoy further rites before Leif's own people, but, until then, we'd celebrate together.

Eirik's gaze had not wavered as he'd made his promise to keep me as a husband should—to care for me, feed and clothe me, protect me, and give me children. The last he'd spoken with a smile, which I'd returned even as my heart trembled, aware of the babe growing already in my womb.

With two pigs and a goat offered in sacrifice to Odin, the animals had been promptly carried off for roasting. The feast couldn't begin in earnest until the meat was cooked. There had been merriment at the tables nonetheless, each set with the abundance of our mid-summer harvest, and every guest given a loaf baked in the shape of a sun wheel.

Though Eirik had desired our marriage without delay, we'd chosen to wait some seemly time, and to conduct our festivities to coincide with *lithasblot*—giving thanks to Urda for the bounty of Svolvaen's lands. The weather had been kind in ripening the crops and, thanks to the algae I'd discovered in the cliff caves, we'd cured the ailment that had plagued our people. We were strong enough again to tend the fields. The first fruits were gathered, and the livestock were faring well.

"There. All done, and 'tis like a golden cloak, my Lady." Setting aside the comb, Sylvi knelt to retie my slippers. They, too, were new, crafted from softest leather and sewn to match my bridal garb.

It felt strange, still, to have others wait upon me. For so long, I'd been little more than a thrall—first as the plaything of Eirik, brought from the shores of my homeland for his pleasure, and then at the mercy of his brother, Gunnolf, in those dark days of Eirik's absence. In name, I'd been 'free', but there had been few choices before me.

Alvis, the lad who tended our livestock, fetched water and firewood, while Sylvi and Guðrún attended to household tasks. I'd helped them even while caring for Asta had been my primary duty. There was always much work to be done—cleaning hare for the pot, kneading bread, churning milk for cheese and butter, smoking and salting meat and fish. We'd be busy preserving for weeks to come. As the jarl's wife, I'd be spared the more burdensome tasks, but I wished to be useful, and neither spinning nor weaving were among my accomplishments.

Another roar of laughter rose from within the hall. I sighed, somewhat wearily, knowing that the revelry would continue long.

Sylvi smiled. "Has been too long since there was merriment. We must let them have their fun."

She was right, of course, but I was reluctant to face again the men's rowdy jests and foolery. The door of the longhouse was wide open this night, and it would be easy for me to slip out, just for a while.

Eirik had given me a wedding gift—a cape of finely woven cloth, trimmed with the russet pelt of a fox. I draped this about my shoulders, glad of it as I stepped out from the warmth of the longhouse. A breeze shivered the forest leaves.

Though the dark hours were few at this time of year, the true night was upon us now. Further down, by the harbor, shone the distant light of torches. Even tonight, the watch kept guard. They'd be impatient at their posts, waiting to be relieved, that they might join the carousing.

I walked some way up the hill, eager to leave behind the unruly celebration. It was my habit to seek the evening air, for I was often disturbed by fretful dreams, and they'd plagued me much of late.

Perhaps that explained my tiredness. I breathed deeply, willing myself to let go my fears. Eirik and I were married, and nothing could prevent our happiness. Soon, I'd tell him of the babe, and he'd want to believe that it was his.

Yet, something gnawed within me. I knew not what the gods of my new home would make of my falsehood, but the omniscient God of my old life would not approve. In my heart, nor did I.

I looked skyward, as if seeking the answer there, and the clouds parted to show me the moon. Full and low hung, it filled the sky with light. But, no sooner had the orb revealed itself, than a shadow passed over. From this, a skull seemed to form, the jaw open in a leering grin. I wanted to look away, but the vision held me transfixed.

Never before had I seen such a thing, though I knew the summer skies were said to play tricks in the same way as the winter borealis.

The next moment, from the corner of my eye, I saw some movement, or heard a footfall, but whoever was there was quicker than me. A hand of steel closed about my throat, while another clamped over my mouth. My shriek of protest came to naught. I was dragged from where I stood, my feet skimming the grass.

It's just a prank! One of Eirik's men come to carry me back.

Except it could not be, for whoever this was, his handling of me was far too rough. He made no attempt to speak, and we were not heading toward the longhouse but away, in the direction of the forest.

I lashed out, jerking my elbow hard into his ribs. His fingers were still pressed to my mouth, and I bit them, only to have my head shoved back violently for my trouble.

"Try that again, and I'll snap your neck." His eyes were cold; his face one I'd never seen before—a face without emotion.

A scream drew my attention back down the hill.

The turf of the longhouse was alight. There were perhaps thirty men, some still tossing their torches upon the roof and through the door.

It had happened so fast. I'd walked outside and had seen no one.

The night was filled with desperate shouts. Those who emerged from the longhouse were in no state to defend themselves. As they fell to the ground, gasping for breath, their attackers' weapons were already drawn.

"No!" My warning was muffled by the hand that held me fast, fingers digging into my cheeks.

There was a rushing, crackling sound as the timbers beneath the turf caught light. Large chunks of the outer covering fell into the space below. The oil-soaked torches tossed upon our home had made quick work. The whole sky seemed to burn.

Eirik!

I saw him, and Helka too, coughing through the billowing smoke. The hem of Helka's gown was alight. Eirik threw her to the grass and rolled her, sprawling across to stop the flames. He did not see the man who approached, who stood over him with a raised sword. In his wedding finery, none could doubt my husband's status. He was the Jarl of Svolvaen.

Terror struck my heart. In the horrible glow, the man's skin appeared red and puckered. His face was framed by a mane of hair that glinted bronze. With both hands, he brought his blade high and plunged it downward, piercing Eirik's body.

I screamed so loud, that even the iron hand upon my mouth could not silence my cry.

The brute placed his foot on Eirik's back, levering upward to withdraw his sword, then kicked him over so that Eirik's eyes were upon the stars. If those eyes were still capable of seeing, I couldn't tell.

Eirik! You must get up!

The sob that rose in my throat choked me.

I must go to him. Help him.

I struggled again, knowing I had to get free. Though my arms were pinned, I kicked back against my captor's shin. He spat a curse and wrenched me about, letting go only to slap me hard across the cheek.

The world spun, and I felt the brute's shoulder in my belly. I tried to raise my head, to make Eirik hear me, but there was no breath in my lungs. I could see nothing through my tears.

We were heading away from the settlement, skirting along the edge of the trees, down toward the meadow. We cut through branches that tore at my hair, pushing on, until I heard the river.

Deposited on my feet once more, I found my knees wouldn't hold me.

I couldn't think, couldn't move. Nothing made sense.

If they would only leave me, I would curl up under the trees and close my eyes. Perhaps it wasn't real. If I went to sleep, wouldn't I wake later and find it all to have been a horrible dream?

But I wasn't to be left. There were four boats sitting low in the glimmering water. Men were slithering down the bank and jumping aboard. I slid over half-rotten leaves before being swung over the side of the last vessel and shoved into the bow.

This was how they'd come, unseen, but from where? And for what purpose? To capture me? It made no sense. To destroy Svolvaen? We'd harmed no one. To plunder our stores? They'd taken nothing.

The boat was near full, and those closest surveyed me. One, whose eyes were gentler than the rest, inclined his head in my direction. "What's this, brother? We were told to take no one. He'll break your arm for it, or your neck."

"None of your business, Thoryn." My captor sneered. "Besides, there's different rules for me. I do as I like."

The other man frowned.

"Cast away. We're done." The call came from the front.

The one who sat beside me brought a length of twine from under the seat, and I watched mutely as he bound my hands.

"Say a word or give me any trouble, and I'll sling you over." He pulled the final knot tight.

I looked back, hoping I would see Eirik—wanting to believe he was unharmed and had managed, somehow, to follow.

But he was not there. There was no one in the trees above us. The breeze carried only a distant wail.

5

ELSWYTH

July 31st, 960AD

I saw only the dark shape of the boats, and the men crouched before me, pulling steadily. We passed through meadows until the flatlands became hills, and the river wound through a wooded valley. More than once, the boats became stuck in the muddied shallows, and all hands were needed to jump over and push us free.

I was alone, and those I loved were dead. Svolvaen's people were not mine by birth, but they had become my family. My hands grew quite numb from the rope, but I did my best to pull my cloak about me.

There was no place to lay down nor any soft place to rest my head. Nevertheless, the constant splash of the oars lulled me, and I dozed. We were passing through a gorge of steeply rising rock when I woke. The river was narrower than ever. Here, the trees grew on both sides, their roots entwined with the looming stone. Where the branches hung low, the men stilled their oars. We hunched over, while the vessel glided silent beneath the foliage.

The moon had faded within a sky of lifting violet. Looking up, I saw that we were followed, but not by human eyes. A pack of wolves leapt over the crags above. Fortunately, there was other prey. Only winter drove them to reckless hunting.

At last, the chasm opened on one side, and the forest came down to meet us, bringing the sound of birdsong and the rustle of small creatures moving beneath the ferns. The men had hardly exchanged a word in all our journey, but they seemed to grow easier, smiling to one another—glad, I supposed, to be not far from their beds.

The sun rose steadily, and my lips grew parched. My captor drank his pouch dry and refilled it from the river but pushed me away when I indicated my thirst. Only Thoryn offered me water, which I gulped gratefully until the other man snatched it away. He knotted a second rope, which he looped about my neck. Weary to the bone, I made no struggle. What little fight remained within me I'd conserve for when I needed it.

Soon, the tree line gave way to meadows once more, and a landscape I would have found beautiful in other circumstances. Beyond the fields and orchards were jagged peaks, but the northern vista was open to the sea. There came the familiar cry of gulls and the tang of salted air.

When the first vessels threw their ropes ashore, the men disembarked without delay. One stood taller than the rest, his hair dark red and wild, reaching past his shoulders. As he turned, a new wave of sickness engulfed me. The left side of his face was puckered with coarse scars. It was the man who'd killed Eirik.

Instinctively, I ducked low, not wishing him to see me, for nothing good could come from drawing the attention of one so brutal.

My captor waited until all others had left our boat before lifting me onto the platform. Tugging on the rope about my neck, he led me uphill, letting the others outpace us.

Soon, the full fjord became visible below—a strip of glittering silver with mountains dominating its far side. The settlement sprawled the width of its harbor. Many of the men peeled away, downward to those dwellings, but we continued to climb, with the forest some way off upon our left.

Ahead of us was a large homestead, surrounded by pens and byres for livestock. A horse was being led from its stable. Women were hanging fish in the smokehouse, and churning butter in the dairy. From one building came the distinctive smell of skins being tanned—rich and earthy, and slightly sweet. From another, a blacksmith's hammer rang clear.

It seemed unreal to me that the heart of Svolvaen had been destroyed, and my own with it. Yet here life continued as normal.

I expected us to approach the longhouse, for I would be just a thrall, brought to serve. If I were lucky, I'd be permitted something to eat and drink, at least, before being given work to do.

"Not there." Seeing the direction in which I looked, my captor tugged harder on the rope, guiding me onward.

There was another hut, high on the headland, set apart. Coming closer, I saw that it commanded a view not only of the fjord and the town but the far mountains and the open water, scattered with small islands. It was a watchpoint, with a brazier upon a great pole, ready to be lit in warning.

Three men sat, their weapons laid to one side, intent on some game. They looked up as we approached.

"What's this, Sweyn?" called one. "Entertainment?" He grinned.

Sweyn merely grunted and gave the door a kick. I hesitated but he jerked me over the threshold. I swallowed a sob. My legs threatened to collapse beneath me, and my neck was rubbed raw. I was hungry, thirsty, and more than a little frightened. I'd no wish to be alone with this man.

The light from the open door revealed a bench along one side and a large chest, with bedding piled in one corner. Sweyn pulled on the rope, hand over hand, until there was no distance between us.

His face contained delighted cruelty. "Fine clothes for a fine lady. Shall we find out if you're just as fine underneath?"

He slipped his hand inside the wide neck of my gown, and his calloused fingers were coarse across my skin. He was taking possession of what he now thought was his. Finding my nipple, he pinched it.

I tried to twist away, but the rope around my neck made that impossible. I stood very still, aware of the sourness of his breath. Despite my fear, I tried to speak forcefully. "Why did you come to Svolvaen? Why did you take me?"

"Because I could. What does it matter?" With a leering smile, he removed his hand, then snapped, "Take it off. I want you naked when we're fucking."

"I won't."

Grasping my face, he turned it upward. "We'll take this outside. You won't be so haughty when you've three holding you down. I'm a generous man. Once I've filled you, they can each take their turn. Then we'll see if you're worth keeping alive."

"No!" The word emerged strangled, and he laughed, his eyes alight with malicious mirth.

I was alone, with no one to help me; no one to care whether I lived or died. And I wanted to live. Not just for the sake of the child I carried, but for myself.

If I could run fast enough, past the men outside, I might reach the homestead. There, someone would take pity on me. I'd be at their mercy, but the women of the house wouldn't let them use me as a whore. This I told myself, summoning what strength remained inside me. Knowing I'd have only one chance, I drew up my knee.

Sweyn must have sensed my intention, for he recoiled as I acted, managing to turn half away, so that I caught him only partially in the groin. Still, it was enough to wind him. Cursing, he released me and staggered backward.

With a hammering heart, I ran, lifting my hem to avoid falling. But I must have misjudged, for the doorway grew dark and I collided with a hard wall. A wall standing three heads above me, wearing a leather breast plate, and with an axe hanging from its belt. A wall of pure muscle, whose hands grasped my shoulders.

I lost all power to move.

It was the demon, his wild hair a fiery mane. The side of his face was scarred. His left eye had barely healed. The burns were recent but, long ago, some blade had cut deep across his cheek, leaving a gash through his beard.

Unblinking, he looked down at me, and I was drawn into his eyes. Even in that dim light, I saw how unusual they were—green and gold. There was power in that gaze. I felt that he might demand anything, and others would obey.

As if he were unsure that I was real, his grasp tightened. His voice rose deep from his chest, rasping. "I commanded that there be no prisoners."

I couldn't see the brute I'd been fleeing from, but I heard the shuffle of his feet.

"The gods threw her easily in my path, Jarl. They meant for me to take her."

In reply, the red demon touched the ivory brooch on the bodice of my gown. He surveyed the rope about my wrists and the thick noose hanging from my neck. "Take as many bed thralls as your cock needs, Sweyn, but not this woman."

My heart beat strangely. Was I to be saved, after all? Those eyes, so intense, did not turn from mine.

"It is I who will own her—for I am owed a debt."

6

ELSWYTH

August 1st, 960AD

I received a mug of buttermilk, which I gulped down greedily, and a hunk of bread. With my hunger appeased, my will was restored.

More than once, I'd faced death, but still I was here. If the gods had a plan for me, I was ready to hear it. For some reason, I'd been brought into the hands of this murderer—the man who'd killed my husband, who must have ordered the torching of our longhouse.

The remembrance filled me with a desire to empty my stomach, but I needed to be stronger than that. The sorrow that filled me was already turning to anger; a more useful emotion to harness, for it might keep me alive.

The jarl commanded that I be washed, and so I was brought to the bathhouse. The two thralls had not looked at their master as he gave them his orders, nor did they wish to look at me, at first.

The hut contained a deep wooden tub, braced like a barrel. A cauldron hung above the fire, its long spout allowing water to be tipped into the bath. The indulgence had not been intended for me—of that I was certain; nor the linens and fine soap, set alongside.

The two women helped me to undress and to climb the steps, holding my hands as I lowered myself into the steaming water. Gradually, they grew braver, and I saw them glance one to the other and back to me.

Without doubt, they were noting the distinctive curve low on my belly. Eirik had thought me only to be eating well, but I could see they knew better.

I must gain their trust. Perhaps they'll know a way for me to escape. Or, if I remain and live long enough to see this babe's birth, they might find a place of safety for the child.

I didn't want to think of that. I couldn't think of it—for such a thing seemed too distant and too sad with all that had happened in the past day and night.

But I needed them, so I smiled as they scrubbed my back and tipped my head for them to wash my hair. I murmured my thanks, asking their names and from where they'd come. They only shrugged at that. Both had been born here—Thirka and Ragerta—and had been slaves, always.

The name of this place? Skálavík.

I fought down my fear. Only two days ago, Eirik had told me his tale, of the dark deeds of Beornwold of Skálavík. But this jarl, the demon, wasn't Beornwold.

I wracked my memory. Some time ago, I'd listened as Gunnolf had plotted the alliance that would strengthen Svolvaen. Eirik had suggested marriage between Helka and the new jarl of Skálavík. She'd protested vehemently, but Gunnolf had dismissed the idea in any case; the jarl was newly wedded, he'd said.

That was something! If I might speak with his bride, she'd be sure to take pity on me—for I'd lost so much. Any person with a heart would feel my pain. I would ask about her when I had the chance. But first, I wished to know more of my enemy, of the man who'd wrought destruction on all I loved.

"The Beast, they call him—*Aifur*," said Ragerta. "Though his birth-name is fearful enough."

"The mountain of fire—that's what it means, Eldberg." Thirka dropped her voice low, as if saying it would conjure him in the room.

"And what has he done to earn this reputation?" I turned the soap over in my hands, pretending a nonchalance I did not feel.

Ragerta glanced at the door. "They say he was taken by berserkers as a boy and raised among them as a slave—but that his bravery earned him his freedom and he fought among them for a while."

"You've heard of those men who are more like beasts?" added Thirka. "They wear only the pelt of bears or wolves and live like them, in the forest."

"They can even jump through fire without being harmed." Ragerta's eyes were wide.

"He claims he can do that?"

"No. He never speaks of that life." Ragerta shifted uneasily, her eyes darting away. "Only once did I hear a man mention this—a merchant, years ago, before Eldberg became jarl. He made some joke, about him going into the forest not to hunt wild animals but to mate with them."

"What happened?" Part of me did not wish to know, but still I listened.

"It was as if he were possessed." Her voice grew quieter. "So great was his rage, I thought he might turn into a true beast before us."

"His teeth!" Thirka added. "He bared his teeth as if to bite."

"And the merchant?"

"I've never seen anyone more frightened. He fled, but Eldberg followed him outside." Thirka pushed her fist to her mouth.

I looked to Ragerta, encouraging her to finish the story.

She bit her lip, adding quickly. "When he came back, he was holding something small, which he threw to the dogs."

I swallowed back a sudden taste of bile. It was a foul thing, to desecrate a body.

"His boat became Eldberg's, of course," said Thirka.

The next moment, I felt a draught upon my back, and the two women shrank away.

Hugging my knees to my chest, I kept very still. Though I couldn't see him, I heard the heaviness of his tread and felt his presence behind me.

Thirka and Ragerta scurried to depart.

"Stand up." That rasping voice again, the words spoken abruptly, expecting to be obeyed.

I didn't reply, nor did I move.

It took but two steps for him to reach me. He placed his hand against the nape of my neck, and my heart leapt in my chest. He was not merely a stranger touching my bare skin, but the man I'd watched murder my husband—a man I had every reason to hate.

I was too afraid to look at him, nor did I wish to comply, but what should I do? Could I reason with such a man?

Before I had the chance to decide, the pressure on my nape increased. Slowly, he raised me up. My feet floundered to gain purchase while my hands flew to where he grasped me, but there was no fighting his strength. Water streamed from my hair and down my body.

My humiliation was immediate, and I brought my hands to cover myself.

He turned me to the firelight. "You will look at me."

The room was warm with steam, yet I shivered.

He studied me—not my body but my mouth, nose, and eyes. His brow drew tight in concentration. "You look like someone..." His voice trailed away. "Yet you are not of Skálavík; nor of Svolvaen."

"I come from Holtholm, far to the west. My husband and his men sought haven with us in a storm and I returned willingly to Svolvaen." I held my chin a little higher. "Is it your habit to kidnap women from your allies and burn their villages? I saw you! You didn't give Eirik a chance to stand. He didn't even know who was attacking him."

"It was no plan of mine to abduct you. That notion was Sweyn's alone. But the gods have brought you to my hands, just as they brought the good fortune of my finding all Svolvaen gathered in one place. I wished a man dead, and he is. I regret only that his passing was too swift. As for this husband of yours, I hear you were thrall to his brother as soon as you were left to your own devices."

His statement shocked me into silence. Dropping my head, I felt the shame of those dark days. My sins still wrenched my heart. Even becoming Eirik's bride, I'd failed to speak honestly. I'd made no confession of my fear that the child I carried was Gunnolf's.

I curled my arms tighter about my body. "You broke our treaty of peace. For what reason?"

Eldberg's reply was pure ice. "You see my face, caused by the assassin your jarl sent to Skálavík."

"My husband wished for peace. He would never have—"

Eldberg cut me off before I could say more. "I speak of Jarl Gunnolf's order, which robbed me of my bride and unborn child."

His wife and child? Dead?

In his last days, a strange madness had overtaken our former jarl. He'd trusted no one. He'd been violent and cruel, even to those who wished to serve him. Could he have sanctioned some terrible deed?

But Eirik bore no guilt for his brother's action.

I began to explain, but Eldberg lunged toward me.

"It changes nothing!" With each word, he shook me. "Your husband did naught to curb his brother's evil—and for that, he deserved death. His kin took what I held most dear, and I shall repay in kind. His end was quick, but your punishment shall unfold at my leisure."

I sobbed, for he was crushing me painfully.

"You are nothing now but my slave and shall serve in my bed—willing or not—until you call me your master."

"Never!" I raised my hand to strike him, but he caught my wrist and twisted back my arm.

I cried out.

My instinct was to escape his hold—to flee, though there was nowhere for me to go. I was naked and friendless. Could I submit as he asked? Every beat of my heart protested. I was to be kept in fear, knowing that any dissent would bring worse punishment.

"I beg your mercy. Know that I plead not just for myself but for the child I carry. It is innocent and should not be punished."

Releasing me, he stepped back and, this time, it was my body that received his appraisal by the firelight's glow: my breasts, then my belly, lingering between my legs, and down their length.

With a mocking smile, he cupped beneath my breast, measuring its weight and smoothness, grazing my nipple with the coarse print of his thumb. His other hand, he laid across my womb. His touch was gentle, but I shuddered. Tears pricked my eyes as I stood helpless.

I'd withstood much—marriage to my pig-of-a-husband in Holtholm, submission, even at Eirik's hands in the earliest days; torment in the long months of his absence when Gunnolf had become my lover. Couldn't I bear this, too?

There was a dark glint in Eldberg's eyes as he moved his hand lower, brushing my fur. His finger parted me, and I flinched. Slowly, he pushed inside.

I turned, not wishing him to see my face, but he growled, commanding me by that feral sound to meet his eyes.

They were filled with shadows, and something far more consuming than lust.

His voice was a cruel whisper, even as he curled his finger inside my flesh. "Perhaps in the spring, I'll take you to Kaupang or Hedeby and sell you in the slave market. Some rich old man would buy you and the child—or one of the higher-class brothels. I might find a trader from one of the eastern harems; they prize a pale complexion, and hair such as yours."

He wouldn't!

But of course, he would. What did he care?

Withdrawing his hands, he brought them to my cheeks. "Or in payment for my murdered child, should I not kill this baby when it's born?"

God help me, and Freya, too!

Whether I allow it or not, he'll take what he wants. If I please him, might I gain favor? Perhaps even my freedom?

The fight left me. For now, I'd do as he asked, and I would endure.

"I'll submit to whatever you command, if you will harm neither myself nor my child." I made myself hold his steely gaze.

He smiled then, and I felt a wave of sickness. I knew not to what I'd agreed.

7

ELDBERG

August 1st, 960AD

The woman clutched the linen to her chest as she rubbed herself dry, attempting to cover her nakedness. He could tell she was trying not to cry.

Three months had passed, and the pain was forever etched on Eldberg's soul. He felt it constantly. The darkness. The despair.

He lived for only one purpose now.

Revenge.

He'd torched Svolvaen and cursed them all to Hel; yet still the venom flowed through his veins.

Elswyth passed the dress over her head; so very like Bretta's had been on the day they'd wedded.

Something about this woman made him uneasy. Was this Loki's trick, or had Sweyn simply seen the likeness? It was why he'd taken her, surely. The same silken hair, falling thick over her shoulders, the same upward tilt of her eyes, the same indented curve to her upper lip. More than that, the way she moved her hands and tilted her head.

She was an echo of the wife lost to him. Coming upon her in the watch house, seeing her in that half-light, just for a moment, he'd thought it was Bretta found again, not dead at all.

The reality of it had brought a hammer blow—as if he'd not suffered enough of those. Not his wife, but that of his enemy, delivered into his hands.

Ah, yes. Odin had presented him with the opportunity for a different sort of revenge. The possibilities were almost overwhelming.

She knew it, too.

His enemy's most prized possession at his mercy, becoming his willing thrall. He could destroy her in a single night if he wished or in a single hour. But there were sweeter paths to the end he sought.

Piece by piece, he would reduce her, until she submitted to him as she never had to her husband. Fearing the worst treatment, she'd be grateful for what she received, and he would offer not just the torment of anticipated pain, but pleasure, too.

She was standing in the wedding dress donned for his enemy— waiting for him, Eldberg, to command her. Given time, he would make her yearn and plead. He would make her beg for him. He would make her betray what she thought she believed.

This would be his true vengeance.

The air was thick with the smell of roasting boar; a feast for the returning men—in reward for a mission well-accomplished. Eldberg let them see his prize, leading her by the rope Sweyn had tied around her neck.

A hush fell amidst the revelry, as they watched their jarl compel his acquisition to the far end of the longhouse.

The partition was but a curtain. Would she appreciate how his men were thinking at this moment? A new woman was always of interest. A new thrall always a possibility, and a temptation.

He would make it clear that she was his— that, for the time being, he forbade any to touch her. But she would not know it. Let her fear and feel his mercy at the same time.

Out of sight, the noise from the feasting continued: laughter and lewd comments beyond the divide that separated his chamber from the rest of the hall.

Eldberg meant to begin immediately. How she spent her first hours would set the tone for what was to come.

He might let her spend the night upon the floor, her ankles and wrists bound, the noose tight around her neck, attached to a hook on the wall. The thought of seeing her like that sent a jolt to his groin, but there were other ways to make her suffer—not like a dog beaten and chained.

When he requested that she remove her clothing, he received no argument. Eldberg took a bolt of jade silk from his trunk. It was among the finery he'd traded on his last trip to Hedeby. Silk he'd bought as a gift for Bretta, that she'd never had the chance to sew into a gown—kept in Sigrid's chamber.

He gestured to Elswyth that she might lay her clothing over the trunk. He'd remove it later, so that she'd know she had nothing with which to cover herself. That privilege would have to be earned.

She brought her arms about her breasts, as if to comfort herself, but did nothing to cover between her legs. He made a point of looking at that part of her as he tore the silk into strips. The fibres gave way easily, ripping along the weft—his destruction of something that had been beautiful.

He motioned with his head again for her to lay upon the bed, to stretch out her arms and legs, to expose herself to him, so that nothing was hidden.

His palm met hers briefly as he tied his first knot. Her hands, small and graceful, clenched into fists. She watched wide-eyed, disbelieving then resigned as he tied her with the silk—each wrist, each ankle. At last, she cast her gaze to the rafters.

How pale she was. Her hair clung damp to her skin—tendrils over each breast. Her nipples, large discs of pink, made his mouth dry. If he took the rosebuds between his teeth, tongued and suckled, would she moan in the same way as Bretta had done? Would she push forward, needing him to take her softness deeper into his mouth, needing him to take possession of her?

He knew the answer to that.

As his captive, she could do nothing to prevent him from taking her body, but she could withhold her mind. For his revenge to be complete, he wanted that, too.

There were many ways in which he could subdue her but, for now, he'd give her something to think about.

"Look at me." He leaned close enough that she would feel his breath on her face—close enough that his leather jerkin brushed her breast. She would be aware of his weight—would know that he could crush her simply by shifting his body over hers.

Still, she looked at the timbers.

He guided her chin downward, until she permitted their eyes to meet. He spoke softly, letting each word unfurl. "One day, soon, you'll give me everything."

Showing her the last strip of silk, he placed the width over her eyes.

She pressed her lips together, saying nothing as he secured it. Only when he brought his hands to rest on her ribcage did she respond with a shuddering breath. Her pulse quickened. She trembled.

What was she imagining?

That he would fuck her?

In this position, lying open, she could be certain of it.

What if he told her something else?

That he would send his men, their fingers greasy from the meat. That he would watch them raising up her hips to meet their thrusts— one by one, until he decided her punishment was enough.

She would believe it.

Her chest rose and fell, and she swallowed, worrying at her lips. She shifted, testing the bonds. They were not so firm that she couldn't move. One foot flexed. She stretched her fingers, then curled them closed again.

He told her nothing, knowing she would tell herself far more.

Eldberg had offered up daily sacrifices to the gods, and they'd looked favorably upon him. The scarring would remain, but he'd kept all the fingers on his left hand. The rest was superficial. Even where his hair and beard had been scorched, there was regrowth.

Still, the pain tested him—strange prickles where the tissue was knitting together. The eye on that side continued to trouble him. The eyelashes were gone, replaced by blistered skin. Some vision remained but, with the eye half-closed, it was difficult to judge distance. When he grew tired, even his own hands refused to come into focus.

If the others knew, none had spoken of it.

If Sweyn or any other had thought to usurp him, they'd waited too long to act upon that ambition. Those closest served through fear but also respect. Who among them would dare claim themselves his rival, fit to take his place?

They hadn't expected him to pick up his weapons. Not yet. Nor had they expected him to lead the attack on Svolvaen. He'd pushed himself to do both—to show them that he was tenacious; a man whose life-force burned stronger than the flames sent to consume him.

This evening, Eldberg was plagued with sparks of pain down his side. In answer, he drank more mead than sat well in his stomach and let the carousing continue longer than he'd intended.

Fiske and Hakon tried to draw him into conversation, avoiding any questions about the woman, though their curiosity was evident.

Sweyn said nothing, sitting apart, unable to hide his scowl.

Eldberg let it pass. The man was entitled to nurse his discontent— as long as he didn't show outright disrespect.

It was a trial to sit so long, knowing she lay in his chamber, but the waiting would do his work for him. Only when most of the men had passed out on the long benches did he return.

The wick had burnt low, but the light was sufficient for him to see her slender body, pale as moonlight. Stretched out on the sheepskins, she occupied the bed he would have thrown himself into had he been alone.

At the sound of his footstep, she twisted against the restraining silk.

Her shoulders were probably aching, though he'd tied her flat and given enough slack to allow her to flex her elbows.

He stood beside her, letting her feel his presence. She would soon know the smell of his body and the rhythm with which he breathed.

She raised her head, and he thought for a moment she would say something, but she lay back again.

His cock grew hard. His body remembered the satisfaction of entering a woman.

In the hours that had passed, he'd had time to plan. From the trunk, he drew out the smaller of the marble columns and the harness that went with it. The leather straps were stiff, being new. Another gift for Bretta—one she'd never seen. He rubbed his thumb over the stone.

A strange thing, he'd thought it, but the merchant who'd sold him the device assured him that the noblewomen of the southern Mediter-ranean all used them. There were five pieces of marble, each slightly wider and longer than the last, chiseled, then polished smooth. Only the final rod bore any resemblance to his own organ, but the trader had explained the thinking behind the progression.

Something about it had aroused him—the idea of watching Bretta touch the thing against that part of her that was designed for his plea-sure. Watching her push the cold stone inside her warmth—moving it in and out and thinking all the while of what she really wanted instead.

That she'd desired him, Eldberg had never doubted. He'd served Beornwold for over ten years before the old man had settled the contract. In that time, Eldberg had watched Bretta grow from a child to a woman, and he'd seen how she admired him. Shyly at first, for she'd been innocent. Later, with an intensity that spoke of the passion she would bring to her husband's bed.

He'd waited, taking no other in marriage, making himself indispensable to the old man. There was no one stronger, no one more formidable, no one better able to take command of Skálavík. Once Beornwold had realized that, the settlement had been straightforward.

And Bretta—so beautiful, so eager, and so in love—had been his.

Eldberg frowned. Always, it came back to this—what had been his, and what had been taken from him.

Moving to the bed, he pressed directly to the crux of fur between the woman's legs.

She jolted with the suddenness of it. Her belly, softly rounded, moved rapidly with her breaths. His touch was abrupt, and his hand cold, no doubt. Nothing cold about the flesh which yielded to the pad of his thumb. There, it was hot.

A subtle shift located her swollen nub.

Just like this, he'd given Bretta pleasure—with his fingers and his tongue.

Dipping inside, he brought out her cream and rubbed lightly upon that part she would be incapable of controlling. She wrenched away, but then her hips pushed forward, meeting the caress again.

His captive.

He played the game patiently, letting her resist with murmured protest, withdrawing, then bucking toward him until the wetness covered not just his fingers but her thighs.

Something inside him tightened. Splaying her with one hand, he touched the marble rod against her slickness.

"What is it?" She tensed.

"It's what you agreed to, slave." With a single push, he slid the column inside her.

"I don't want it." She thrashed her hips, then bore down, trying to expel the thing that filled her.

"An ungrateful way to behave when you've been given a gift."

As she raised herself again, attempting to shake away the rod, Eldberg slipped the leather harness under her back. His fingers were not as nimble as they had been, and the wick had all but burnt away, but he didn't need his vision to fasten the strap around her waist.

"What are you doing?"

In the near dark, he wedged the rod into its leather cup and brought the holding straps over her lower abdomen, knotting them onto the front of the belt. These, he pulled tight, so that the marble shaft was drawn fully into her body, held securely in place.

"I don't want it!" she hissed again. "When I move..." She made an exasperated sound, then lay still.

Satisfied, he pulled one of the sheepskins from the bed and tossed it on the floor. She'd have all night to simmer.

In the morning, he'd ease her discomfort—at least for a little while.

"Take it out," she said quietly. "Please."

He smiled.

"Pleading already?"

8

ELSWYTH

August 1st, 960AD

I imagined all the ways I might kill him. A blade through the heart or sliced across his neck. Perhaps an axe through his skull, or a swift-acting poison. Even beating him to death with the thing he'd left inside me.

When I tilted my hips, it sent an ache of yearning through my sex. It was provoking and demeaning in a way I couldn't put into words.

And how long was I to be tied?

The restraints only chafed when I struggled, so I lay still and tried to divert my thoughts.

I'd agreed to obey him for the sake of the babe I carried, and for my sake, too, since I didn't wish to die, but my blood grew feverish.

I'd have my revenge—not just for myself but for Eirik and all Svolvaen.

He was a brute and, whatever he thought, I'd never belong to him.

In his madness, Gunnolf had sentenced Svolvaen to its cruel fate, and we had all paid the price. Eldberg had been wronged, but we weren't to blame, and there was no justice in the retribution he'd brought upon us.

He'd bedded down on the floor, the smell of mead strong on his breath. While I lay awake, he snored.

At last, I must have dozed, for I woke to the dim light of dawn filtering through the smoke hole in the rafters. The man I loathed stood above me, holding the sash that had covered my eyes.

"I need to pass water." I made no effort to hide my scowl. "And drink some," I added with less abruptness. I wasn't in a position to show my temper.

He appeared subdued this morning, his face grey. He said nothing and moved as if he were in discomfort.

A bad head, I hoped, from too much drink. Perhaps his back was stiff from his night on the floor.

He unfastened the belt and straps about my waist first, drawing his hand down my belly, letting his fingers brush my damp curls before pulling out what had tormented me. I couldn't help but gasp as it left my body.

Thank the gods!

Relief, and something else.

I was slightly sore from being stretched, but also very wet. Having held the thing inside me for so long, it felt strange for it to be gone.

With the untying of my wrists, my impulse was to claw at his face, but I wasn't a fool. Whatever state he was in, he remained stronger than me. If I wanted to inflict pain upon him, it would have to wait until I'd better knowledge of this place and an ally to help me escape.

Even with all four limbs free, I couldn't right myself. I rubbed at my wrists, shook them, rotated my shoulders, then my ankles. Everything hurt.

With a grunt, Eldberg raised me to a sitting position and fetched a bowl from the corner.

More humiliation!

A prisoner in this room, tied to the bed, impaled, and made to piss in a pot.

I gritted my teeth, bringing myself to the edge of the bed. Gingerly, I squatted over the bowl.

"Turn away, can't you!" I cast him a black look.

49

He grunted again and called out for Ragerta. She must have been waiting, for she appeared promptly.

"Food and ale for both of us." He passed his hand through his disheveled hair. "Hot water and a cloth."

As I pushed myself back onto the bed, he picked up the pot and passed it to her.

"Get rid of this."

She glanced at me, showing no surprise at my naked state. Of course, she would not. Everyone would know my purpose in the jarl's chamber.

There were voices and movement in the main part of the hall already.

Damn the lot of you.

They were the men who'd burnt Svolvaen. The men who'd carried me away to this place. I hoped the rich food they'd eaten the night before turned their bowels liquid. I hoped they felt as bad as Eldberg looked.

Curling my feet under me, and my arms about my body, I shrank to the corner of the bed.

He sat heavily on the edge, his head in his hands. I thought again about caving in his skull, but I had no weapon—nothing of sufficient weight. The harness and the stone thing were upon the trunk, out of reach.

On Ragerta's return, he took the mug from her and gulped it down, then nodded for her to refill it. Being thirsty, I also drank.

There was porridge—just like the grøt Sylvi used to make, sweetened with honey. I ate hungrily, scraping round with my spoon.

"You don't need to tie me again," I ventured. "You have my oath that I'll do your bidding."

Eldberg wiped his mouth before tossing his bowl away.

"I'll do what pleases you." Leaning forward, I touched his hair gently.

He jerked away, grasping my wrist. One twist and I was flat upon the bed again, his bulk bearing down on me. His other hand came to my throat. "You won't seduce me with lies, thrall."

His thigh came between mine. "I shall know when you truly desire to please me." Releasing his hold on my neck, he took his hand lower, squeezing my nipple hard—making me gasp with the suddenness of it.

"When that time comes, you'll take me into your body and plead for my seed. You'll fuck me all the ways a woman can take a man and the viper in you will writhe for more. You'll ride me until your cunt aches, and still you'll beg."

Pinned beneath him, I seethed. I'd never beg.

He was growing aroused. Through his clothing, he was hard against my stomach. I was all too aware of my nakedness—leather and chain links against my breast and belly, woolen serge between my legs.

Before I had the chance to reply, he flipped me onto my front. With my cheek pressed to the bed, I faced the wall.

"Fuck you!" I couldn't help myself. The man was an animal. Again, he was tying my wrist—looping the silk and knotting it, pulling me forward to secure the sash to the far bedpost.

I could do nothing to prevent him from tying the other hand.

"Please." I couldn't let him do this again. "You don't need to—"

"Quiet, thrall." He dragged my legs apart.

Though none of the bonds were drawn tight and the sheepskins were soft to lie upon, I could not bear the thought of being made to remain still again.

"Don't do this."

And then I felt the warmth of the dampened cloth, drawn gently up my inner thigh. He caressed both sides before dipping it into the water again, then wrung out the excess. Easing apart my cheeks, he drew it along the crease, pressing to my anus.

A trembling fear was taking hold of me—that he would enter me there. I'd felt the size of him when he'd been pressed to my stomach.

He put aside the cloth and rested his palm upon my behind.

"You won't hurt me." My voice sounded so small.

The bed creaked, and I heard the chest lid open. I caught a glimpse of what he withdrew. Another of the stone columns, though larger and carved differently—its head more bulbous, the shaft slightly curved, and studded with protruding nobbles.

"No!" I protested, fighting my tears.

"You agreed to all." He sat again and parted me, though not where I had most feared. Though the stone was cold, it entered between my curls with surprising ease.

I awaited a cruel thrust to the hilt but, to my relief, he proceeded carefully. As it slid inside, I could not help but gasp. My own will counted for nothing.

After some moments, he withdrew it—just as gently, until it left me altogether. It was to be a slow torture; one that amused him despite his ill night's sleep. He rubbed the rounded head where I was swollen: nudging, teasing, before penetrating me again haltingly.

I kept my eyes on the wall and bit my lip.

It would soon be over. Soon.

Next, he twisted it, so that it touched in new ways. He moved his other hand low beneath my belly, and his palm was hot. I drew breath sharply as he extended his thumb to press against my most sensitive place.

I was unable to move or resist as he simulated the act between a man and woman, using the shaft of stone, back and forth, and the pad of his thumb to taunt me.

I pushed into the bed, but he raised me on his palm so that his impalement became deeper. I buried my face in the sheepskins, refusing to let him hear me moan. Despite all I felt—my hatred and humiliation, anger and disgust—I knew what he was coaxing from me. A burning warmth was overtaking all thought. Pain and piercing pleasure were building.

When it broke, the cry tore from my throat.

He left me tied all day, face downwards, but without the harness—without the invasion of his toy. Twice, Ragerta came to hold a cup to my lips, helping me to drink. For my other needs, she slid the pot beneath me.

My chest was tight with refusal to weep.

I'd crossed a threshold, betrayed by my body. Though the secrets of my heart were my own, Eldberg had won some small part of me, and so easily.

I listened to the working sounds of the hall—hushed chatter, and a woman's voice giving orders. From outside, there was the sound of cows and the bleating of ewes. There was hammering, the thud of butter churning, flapping wings, and sudden squawking.

Ragerta brought me the *nattmal* of vegetable broth, spooning it into my mouth with swift efficiency. I asked her if Eldberg had done this before and what had happened, but she merely shook her head without answering, as if worried who might hear her.

Afterward, I lay quietly, knowing he would come soon.

By the time he did, the room was full dark, and he lit the wick in a dish of oil.

He did not come near me at first, and I remained turned away as he undressed. I did not wish to look on him as he removed his clothing, though I sensed his eyes were upon me. I heard the clink of his weapons and the soft fall of his tunic and leggings to the floor.

Much time passed before he said, "Do you wish me to touch you?"

I kept my face turned. "I've agreed to serve you. Whatever happens is your wish, not mine."

It was an insolent answer and ill-advised, but he spoke no threat of punishment. Instead, he untied the sash about one of my ankles and rubbed the skin, his calloused hands firm in their kneading, restoring the flow of blood.

Climbing upon the bed, he removed the restraint from my other leg and caressed it in the same manner.

A lump formed in my throat, but I gave no thanks. Whatever kindness he showed me was for his own ends. Being partially free, I should have felt better able to defend myself, but there was no truth in that. He'd merely gained power to position me in other ways. My hands were still bound, after all.

I resolved to do nothing to help him.

Fuck me, and it shall be as if I were a corpse.

He ran his hands along my calves and thighs, until he clasped my hips.

Leaning forward, he kissed one cheek, then the other. He devoured my flesh with open mouth, sucking and biting—though without force enough to hurt me. All the while, he held my hips fast.

I squirmed but kept silent.

Moving one hand to the small of my back, he used his other to probe my wetness. "You desire this." He pressed with his thumb, circling, teasing. "You want me inside you."

My head buzzed with fury even as I writhed under his caress.

He laughed low. "What have you been thinking of, waiting for me?"

"That you want to torture me. To punish me for something of which I'm innocent."

"Punish you." He withdrew his hand. "Is that what you desire?"

"Nay! That is not what I said!"

He rose from the bed, and I heard the chest's lid open.

I dared not look, but heard the switch pass through the air. The pain was immediate—a burning sting across the crease of my lower buttocks.

"This is what you want, thrall?"

"Nay!" I cried, fearful that he would strike me again.

I attempted to push my thighs together, but his hand intruded upon me. Three fingers slid easily inside. Against my will, liquid rose from deep within the flesh that he sought to make his own.

"You deny this pleasure, but soon, you'll think only of the man who masters you now."

He struck me twice with the switch, across the fleshiest curve of my behind, and the moan from my lips came unbidden.

I abhorred him, yet there was a tug inside me. My body opened to him, despite the rebellion of my mind. To say what he wanted to hear would make all easier, but I could not yet surrender this piece of myself.

I sobbed, burying my face, waiting to be punished again; instead, he smoothed my hair. Without speaking, he untied the final sashes. As I curled away from him, he brought his arm across my body, pulling me into the warmth of his chest.

I was aware of his nakedness, of his arousal pressed to the crevice of my cheeks, but he made no move to force his penetration. I lay, aware of him behind me, his breathing becoming that of a man who slept.

Wearily, I closed my eyes.

I no longer knew myself, nor understood the man who held me captive.

9

ELSWYTH

August 3rd, 960AD

R agerta woke me, helping me sit up, placing a bowl of *grøt* in my hands.

"Where is he?" I hadn't felt him rise from the bed. If he were close by, would he tie me again, now I was awake?

"At the harbor. There's a new trading boat in," she whispered. "But he won't be long." She indicated the pail standing by. "I've water for you to wash. He told me to help you quickly."

"Ragerta." I placed my hand upon her arm, wanting to say something to explain away my shame. It was unnecessary, of course. What did she care? I was her master's bed-thrall, and there was nothing to excuse or judge.

"Thank you," I said simply.

The water was hot and welcome—not as refreshing as the barrel in the bathhouse, but I could hardly expect that privilege, unless it was Eldberg's wish that I be taken there.

"He said I was to watch you." Ragerta gave an apologetic smile.

There was naught for me to do but await his return. He'd take whatever pleasure amused him, I supposed, then leave once more. I could try again to persuade him that he didn't need to restrain me—that I'd be compliant.

This was my best hope, wasn't it? Only if I were free could I hope to escape. Not yet perhaps, but as soon as I had a plan.

But what did compliance mean?

For me to writhe and beg, and disavow the love I'd borne Eirik?

This I still could not bring myself to do; nor did I wish to be a passive slave.

I would invite his passion, but on my own terms.

Ragerta was right; he was not long in returning.

Entering the chamber, he immediately dominated all around him. Ragerta scurried away, leaving us alone.

I'd thought carefully of how I would present myself and what I would say. Already, I'd wasted almost two days and nights. The sooner I made him believe I was pliant, the sooner I might escape.

I lowered myself on the sheepskins, raising my arms and parting my legs in simulation of the position in which he'd tied me.

His gaze was wholly upon my body as I did so, and I felt a new energy fill the room, as if there was nothing else but my nakedness and his desire to possess what he saw.

"You await me, thrall." It was a statement rather than a question, but I nodded, parting my legs a little farther and turning one knee outward, that he might see what I offered him.

Neither of us spoke as he unstrapped the leather at his waist, from which his short-bladed dagger hung. He pulled his tunic roughly over his head and jerked open the drawstring of his trousers, kicking them away.

With the mid-morning sunlight filtering through the central opening in the longhouse roof, I was able to view him as I had not before.

The burns which marred his face travelled the length of his body, but only upon his left side. From his neck they passed across one shoulder and down the muscles of his arm.

Ugly, raised welts broke the contours of his body ink. The scars dappled the hard plane of his chest and the ridges of his stomach, reaching the deep crease of his abdomen and continuing down his thigh, even to his foot.

His arousal was already prominent, springing from the russet hair at his groin. The sight made the breath catch in my throat.

Stepping closer, he took my hand and guided me to encircle him.

Rubbing my palm to his thickness, he said, "Now, you see what I will thrust inside you."

My punishment, and your revenge.

My mouth was suddenly dry.

Will you be happy when this is done?

With his hand over mine, he stroked upward from the root, squeezing hard. It took nothing more for him to become rigid as iron, a bead of moisture glistening at the tip.

He gave one final stroke and released me. "Another day I shall teach you how to take me into your mouth."

To my dismay, he knelt to retrieve his leather belt. Touching my hip, he rolled me to my front. Leaning close, his voice was huskily soft. "Let them hear that I am your master—that you are no longer a woman of Svolvaen, but mine." He nodded to the curtain that divided us from the greater chamber.

My cheeks were still tender from the strikes visited upon me previously.

Was this what it meant—to be owned by the Beast? He meant to flog me with the thick leather which carried his weapons?

Perhaps he heard my gasp, for he looked up.

Holding the strap in his hand, he watched me with curiosity. "This excites you?" He regarded my buttocks and then the belt. "You appreciate pleasure only when tempered with pain?" He appeared to think upon it, rubbing the leather between his fingers.

"I shall first give you pleasure and then we shall see." He extracted a small pouch and then a vial from within.

A potion?

There were such things, I'd heard, that heightened sensation and passion. Only once had I experienced such a thing, when breathing the sacred smoke of Svolvaen's Ostara celebrations. I'd not been myself that night. With my inhibitions lowered, I'd welcomed a coupling that should never have been.

Eldberg came again to the bed, sitting above me.

When he opened the bottle, it brought a strong scent. Ginger and sage? I wasn't sure. Those could be drunk when prepared as a tincture.

"Neroli," he murmured, "and sandalwood: an exotic blend, held in oil. I paid a fine price this morning. You see, thrall, what I do to coax what I desire from you."

It made no sense. He had only to thrust himself between my legs and the act would be done.

He first brought my arms to my sides and tucked my unbound hair above my head. Then, he poured some of the oil into his hands. His movements were firm as he kneaded the knots of tension in my neck and shoulders.

Despite myself, I welcomed his caress.

My tears seemed never far away, and they sprung now—at this unexpected tenderness. I was wound tight with grief not yet expressed, and I thought of Eirik as my captor stroked downward. Never again would my husband's hands worship my body, nor would I be able to show my love in return.

I wanted to hate this man's touch. To feel otherwise was a betrayal but, as his thumbs traced gentle circles upon my spine, I felt some of my tension depart.

When he found the dimples of my lower back, he gripped my waist, and his arousal brushed against me.

I stiffened at that reminder of what was to come, and my heart beat faster. But, he merely continued, rubbing the curve of my hips and the fullness of my cheeks. He worked the fleshiest part, then the crease where my buttocks met my thighs. The fragrant oil aided his movements. His fingers stroked lower, slipping into the cleft of my behind. When he skimmed lower, to my curls, I parted my thighs willingly, wanting the fingertip that he dipped inside.

All the while, I closed my eyes and tried to imagine that it was Eirik who touched me, but I could not deceive myself. These hands were not Eirik's.

At last, Eldberg moved himself over my back, so that his cock nestled where his hands had caressed, between my cheeks. His thigh pushed insistently between my legs, encouraging me to open wider.

He was breathing hard, nudging where he wished to enter.

No! I cannot!

I'd taken a man inside me there before, but Eldberg was bigger than any lover of my past, and I feared what he was capable of—that he might use me too roughly. Suddenly, I feared taking him at all. In the throes of desire, he might tear me asunder.

He shifted, drawing my legs between his own so that he fully straddled my hips.

In that moment, I turned swiftly onto my back. I made myself look at him, saying the words I knew he wished to hear. "You shall own me everywhere"—I brought his hand to my breast—"but, first, caress me."

I wetted my lips. "Spend your seed here, if you wish it, or over my belly. Let me rub you into my skin, that I may smell of you."

His expression was inscrutable. His erection rested on my stomach —a hard rod pressing where there was no entry to be had. Drawing back, he sat on his haunches, his arousal above me. In one swift motion, he took hold of my hips and pulled them to him, so that my sex rested upon his testicles.

I was aware of his manhood—the head dark and swollen, the shaft, thick-veined. It would take only a subtle movement for him to press into my sheath, and ride me there, as deeply as he liked. I would be held fast, and unable to escape.

However, he continued to look at me with eyes half-closed, as he poured more of the oil into his palms. He swept over my belly, circling there, until he gathered my breasts in his hands and moved upon them in the same way. His palms covered then revealed, holding and releasing. With each kneading stroke, my nipples grew hard and tight, aching to be touched more roughly.

Even through my fear, I did not wish him to stop. Beneath the rhythm of his caress, a strange languor overtook me, and a warmth low in my womb.

At last, he brought his mouth where his hands had labored. Gently, he bit, then suckled hard, so that I arched into his hunger. His mouth was fiery hot on my skin, his beard softly grazing. I moaned, even as I was repulsed.

When our eyes met again, his glinted darkly.

His arousal now rested at the opening of my sheath.

I'd known this moment would come, yet I struggled—only to have him capture my wrists and drag them above my head, palm on palm.

Only then did he touch his tongue to my lips.

I cannot! That intimacy is for lovers—not for what exists between us. I'm no more than a body for your pleasure, and for the perverse revenge you think to take.

I twisted away, but he threaded his fingers through my hair. I was helplessly exposed—not just to his cock but to his insistent mouth. He kissed my neck and my jaw, then returned to my lips. Brushing softly, he persisted until I opened slightly to the press of his mouth. His tongue entered tentatively, meeting mine. At the same moment, he nudged his arousal between the soft flesh of my cleft.

In a single stroke, I was breached.

I cried out, though more in shock than pain. My own traitorous arousal had helped him, for I was slippery with need for the sexual act.

He held himself inside me, the soft hair of his chest pressing to my breasts, his breath soft on my cheek. I'd thought to have taken him all, but he pressed forward again, and I realized he was not yet at the hilt.

I bit my lip to keep from moaning. He was so deep.

Easing back, he paused before his second grinding thrust. It came more easily, as did the next.

He lowered his mouth to my nipple, pulling the point into his wet warmth. Once there, he did not release it, consuming and demanding, drawing harder, sending a searing flame to my womb.

I was no longer myself; only the body that he shaped to his whim.

With each driving advance, I responded. I wrapped my feet about his back, and he left my breast to find my lips again. Open-mouthed, I let him kiss me fully, with a terrible, overwhelming need to surrender.

I bucked against each stroke from his smooth length. Submissive to my heightened state, I knew nothing but sensation. It was I who shuddered first, half-sobbing.

This brought on his own release. His features contorted, and his groan was that of a man both conquered and conquering.

With the last throbs of his pleasure, he grew still, and the look upon his face was wretched. I saw there an echo of all I felt: despair and pain, and a chasm of loneliness.

Eirik was dead, and I was slave to this man's bed—as I had been to Gunnolf's. I knew this path and the soulless, aching emptiness that would come.

10

ELSWYTH

August 4th, 960AD

The next morning, it was not Ragerta who brought me food. The woman who swept aside the curtain was no thrall.

"Stand up. Let me see you." I recognized her voice—one I'd heard many times since I'd been brought to Eldberg's chamber. In some manner, she was mistress here, though not his wife, I knew.

The room smelled of coupling: thick with sweat and the scent of sex. Scowling, she pursed her lips, and the lines it brought to her mouth made apparent her age. Her hair, worn in a thick braid, was a similar hue to my own, only slightly lighter at her temples. She bore the expression of one who'd seen too much of life's bitterness. It was etched in her face. Perhaps mine was the same or would soon come to be so.

I rose from the bed, drawing my hair over my breasts and clasping my hands to cover my sex. That part of me was sore, for Eldberg had taken me twice more through the night.

She made no bones of surveying my nakedness, then my face. She stared long and hard at each feature, as if there was some puzzle she wished to decipher. She met my eyes, and something flashed in her own.

"I've no wish to be here," I said quietly. "And I do not remain willingly."

The woman waved her hand in dismissal. "Were it up to me, you'd be thrown from the cliff and that would be the end of you."

Her mouth tightened again, and she frowned. "As it's not my decision, you'll make yourself useful. Not just in here"—she glanced briefly at the bed—"but in other ways."

My heart gave a leap.

I was to escape this confinement.

It would be the first step toward my finding a way to leave this place.

"You can weave, I suppose? You know how to prepare meat, how to make bread and porridge?"

"Yes—all those things." I nodded.

"Then get dressed, and we'll find you work." From a sack at her side, she tossed a bundle of fabric. "It's too fine for a thrall, but he insists you wear it."

It was my own soft undershift and gown—sewn for my wedding day. I held them to my chest. To have me wear the gown as I served in his household was a cruel joke. Yet, I was glad—for it was my own, and wearing it would keep to mind all that I'd lost. It would give me strength to make my escape and have my revenge upon the man who'd inflicted so much suffering.

The woman had not returned my cape. That, with its soft collar of fur, I imagined she'd kept for herself.

"You're not to go outside, and if you give us any trouble, he'll tie you again. Perhaps you'd prefer it, being used for whoring and none of the real work." She sniffed with obvious distaste.

"Nay, I only wish—"

"Don't speak unless I ask you a question!"

The glare she gave assured me I should avoid baiting her temper.

"And keep a civil tongue! Know your place and call me mistress." With that, she swept out.

I shook out the gown. There was dried mud on the hem, which would be easy to brush out. Checking its deep pocket, my fingers closed over what I'd placed there when I'd undressed in the bath-house: the amulet Eirik had gifted to me, depicting Mjolnir, Thor's magical weapon.

Months before, Eirik had left with Helka on their mission to Bjorgyn. He'd placed the amulet about my neck, promising to return. More time had passed than either of us had anticipated, but I'd worn the pendant, always, and he'd kept his word.

Did I dare wear it again?

It no longer had the power to bring him back to me. Nothing could do that. And Eldberg would likely take it from me if he saw it.

Better to leave it where it was.

They were all together now—Eirik, Gunnolf, and Asta.

Helka, too, and Astrid? Were they watching from some other realm? That I could not think about. While I lived, my concerns had to be with this world.

Entering the main hall of the longhouse, I was astonished again by its size—twice that of ours in Svolvaen.

The main door was open wide, and sunlight entered also through the hole in the roof, directly above the fire pit.

In the kitchen area, Thirka was pulling the skin from a hare.

At the far end, fleeces were stacked high, reading for dyeing. Ragerta was spinning carded wool into yarn, while the woman who'd come to me stood at her loom.

She jerked her head toward the fire, which was bounded by high stones. Three iron pots simmered over its flames: one filled with water and the other two with stew. All were suspended by chains, hooked high into the ceiling beams. A grid of iron bars covered one end of the pit, for the roasting of meat.

"When you've finished mooning about, there's bread to knead," called the woman.

The dough had been placed in a wooden trough, and I marveled at the volume: enough to make thirty loaves or more. Soon, my arms and back were aching. I sat on my heels for a moment, straightening up and rolling my shoulders.

"Lazy bitch! I didn't say you could stop!" the mistress called out loud enough for all to hear. "Keep at it, or I'll take the birch to you."

I'd met women like her before—the sort who liked to bully those unable to defend themselves.

"Go and help her, Ragerta, or we'll be waiting 'till midnight." She scowled.

Scurrying to join me, Ragerta knelt alongside. "Here, I'll take one end of the dough, and you the other. Lift as high as you can, fold inward, then push hard into the middle. It won't take much for Sigrid to punish you, so don't give her a reason."

It was much easier together.

"Who is she?" I whispered, aware of hard eyes watching us.

Ragerta rotated the dough, and we lifted it again. Keeping her head lowered, she spoke into the trough. "Sigrid, the old jarl's sister."

"Beornwold's sister?" I glanced over. Part of the warp appeared to be wearing thin on the loom and she was intent on twisting new fibers into the upright thread. "And she's mistress here?"

"Always has been. She's a shrew—never happy—but worse since Bretta died."

Bretta. Eldberg's wife.

Not for the first time, I wondered about her. "What was she like, this Bretta?"

Ragerta paused in her kneading but didn't answer.

She passed over one of the long-handled paddles next to the trough. "Fist-sized pieces," she directed. "Pull them off and roll them in your palm. Sigrid likes them slightly flattened."

Demonstrating, she eased one onto the paddle. "When we've ten loaves on, we'll slide them over the embers."

Again, we worked.

From outside came the sound of cattle lowing—passing in front of the longhouse, being led down to pasture.

"Did he love her?"

Ragerta's eyebrows rose. "We all loved Bretta."

Like Asta.

We'd all loved Jarl Gunnolf's wife.

"But what sort of marriage was it?"

Ragerta stared at me, and I felt my cheeks redden. I didn't know why I was asking.

"Arranged of course. Beornwold had no sons and needed an heir. Eldberg joined him as a paid hand at first, on trips to raid the Western lands. When Beornwold saw his strength, he adopted him, then married him to Bretta. Their offspring would be sure to continue the line."

"Except that she died."

Ragerta frowned. "It was a terrible thing." She seemed to think for a moment, then shook away the image. "Sigrid was mother to her from the start. A bad birthing, you know..."

I did know. I'd seen my share of babes and mothers die. Unconsciously, my hand went to my belly. What if that happened to me? Who would look after this child?

I asked hurriedly, not wanting to lose my chance, "Is there someone you have feelings for, Ragerta? Someone you love?"

"By Freya! What a thing to ask!" Ragerta looked flustered. "There are one or two I let take me outside, and a few I've had to lay with regardless of my choice. I'm not fool enough to think any of it matters. I'm naught to them, nor they to me."

I didn't know what to say. It was a sad thing for any woman to admit.

"Now, ask Thirka, and you might hear a different answer." Ragerta gave a sly smile. "Thoryn's been sweet on her this half-year past, and he's a better sort than most."

We'd almost reached the end of the dough, and the last of the cows had passed the doorway.

"But naught will come of that," I mused. "Not unless Eldberg frees her."

"True. No thrall can marry a free man, so here she'll stay." The loaves being all upon the embers, Ragerta made to rise. "Eldberg has never freed any in his possession. Those who disappoint or anger him, he sells at the slave market—or gives a quicker end."

With that thought in my mind, the room suddenly grew gloomier, the sun falling dim. Looking up, I saw the jarl standing upon the threshold, his breadth and height silhouetted against the light.

"Come." He indicated that I was to enter his chamber.

He wasted no time in stripping away his own clothing, then mine. Throwing me upon the bed, he bound me downward. With him upon my back, I was pinned. His cock nestled between my cheeks, while his legs touched the length of mine. He reached beneath to take my breasts in his hands, kneading them as I had the bread.

"Speak." His arousal nudged where he'd attempted to claim me the night before. "Tell me that you wish this."

"I'm ready for you, my Jarl." It was neither truth nor lie. My fear was potent, but as he'd tied the sashes about my ankles and wrists, the snake had unfurled once more in my belly, hissing its desire.

"And what am I to do with you?"

"Enter me, my Jarl." I closed my eyes as he brought one hand down my belly, then lower, to the tender part of me. I was already swollen and wet. As I moaned for him, his voice rasped. "You please me, thrall."

His fingers pressed to my open slit, while he rubbed his girth between the crease of my buttocks.

"Tell me," he said again.

With my body jarred by the force of his, it was difficult to speak.

"Please," I asked breathlessly. This was what he wanted—for me to beg. "Your seed. Spill inside me, my Jarl."

Slippery, he drew back and with his next stroke, pushed against my tighter place.

Dear gods! My instinct was to clench against the intrusion, but as he played upon my sensitive part, stroking there, the snake inside me writhed in rippling waves.

With its tongue licking hot, I accepted his entry from behind, while his finger penetrated my other place.

I was lashed with the poison of pain and pleasure combined.

11

ELDBERG

August 4th, 960AD

Eldberg tore off the last strip of meat, then sucked the juices from the bone.

He was ravenous; hungry enough to eat another whole trencher of food. Hungry for something else, too, though he'd been consuming that delicacy for the better part of the afternoon.

He watched as she made her way to each guest, seated the length of the hall, either side of the central fire. To celebrate their success in burning Svolvaen, several nights of revelry were planned.

As Elswyth refilled cups with mead, the eyes of every man were upon her. She kept her own lowered. No doubt, she was keen to go unnoticed. As if that were possible!

Her gown's slender bodice and low-cut yoke placed her well on display, letting all see her ripeness. Breasts to make even the goddess Freya envious! Silken to the touch, full and heavy. Nipples of the palest pink, large and soft, until they hardened beneath his tongue.

He'd sated his cock well-enough, but he was hard again, thinking of her tightness and warmth, thinking of how it felt to move inside her. It had been satisfying to watch her struggle, to try to deny him, but he preferred seeing her pliant—submitting to acts she found shameful, yet unable to control her response.

She glanced at him, and he saw her tremble.

Good!

He took a long draught, draining his cup then raising it. Let her come to him.

Eldberg watched the sway of her hips as she walked; hips made for a man to hold onto. She was a fine piece of womanhood, though she behaved more like a virgin—as if she'd never been touched before. It aroused him, her blend of reluctance and passion.

Only when she stood beside him did she look up, her lips parting as she gazed into his face. Those lips! A little plump. A little bruised.

She hadn't wanted to kiss him, but he'd refused to let her get away with that. A thrall obeyed her master. She'd no right to hold anything back.

As she replenished his cup, he brought his hand around her waist. Her scent lifted to him: honey and musk. She squirmed, almost pulling away, but he tugged her closer.

The curve of her breast was before his face. How easy it would be to release that bounty and taste it again. By the gods, he was iron hard! He'd a mind to raise her skirts and haul her onto his lap right here.

"Eldberg!" Sigrid's voice, shrill beside him, intruded. "Did you hear what I said?"

Distracted, he relaxed his hold on Elswyth's waist, and she neatly slipped away.

"What is it, Sigrid? Must you nag me even while I eat?" Eldberg scowled.

No other dared speak to him as Sigrid did. Not for the first time, he berated himself for permitting it. Her shrewish ways made him want to wring her neck, but he owed her a debt. He was a man who never forgot an injury and never forgave an insult, but nor did he ignore the service of those who were loyal.

All those years Beornwold had been without a wife, she'd been lady of this hall, running the household. Moreover, she'd raised his

71

daughter, loving Bretta as any true mother. Only she, of anyone in Skálavík, knew the grief Eldberg had suffered. Without speaking of it, she understood.

He'd not forgotten, either, that she'd tended him through his recovery. The healer had provided salves, but Sigrid had administered them and, through those first weeks, when sleep was impossible without the coming of nightmares, she'd sat beside him.

She deserved a degree of respect and status, and he would not put her from the house, though she oft drove him to the edge of his temper.

Sigrid lowered her voice, but her words were no less scathing. "Are you turning fool? Letting that trollop tame you? You've done little but moon after her since your return."

"If anything is to be tamed, I wish it were your tongue," retorted Eldberg. "Beware, mistress, lest you stretch your neck too far toward my blade."

"Ha!" Sigrid took a swig from her cup. "That is more like the jarl we serve! A man ready to act when one beneath him oversteps the mark."

She placed her hand upon his arm. "Beware yourself, or you'll have Skálavík laughing at your folly—a jarl who forsakes his duties in pursuit of a hussy!"

Eldberg removed Sigrid's hand. "If I require your advice, you shall know of it. Until then, better we sit in silence."

Sigrid tossed her head, ignoring the warning, though she lowered her voice. "You'll see the truth when it stares you in the face. Until then, make your mistakes."

Gritting his teeth, Eldberg motioned over one of the other thralls, stabbing a piece of mutton from the platter.

"And what is it, good aunt, that's clear to everyone else except me!"

Sigrid leaned in closer. "She's a wanton. Good for nothing but opening her legs."

"Is that all the complaint you have of her?" Eldberg barked with laughter. "Why do you care whose cunt I use? She's my bed thrall—nothing more."

Sigrid shifted in her seat. "You agreed she'd help as the others do."

"That she may, when I've no immediate use for her beneath me. If she's lacking, then teach her, but don't grumble to me, Sigrid."

Picking an apple from the bowl, she quartered it with her knife. "As long as she pleases you, 'tis good enough reason for her to stay. I shall say no more about it."

"Odin be praised!" Eldberg went to drain his cup but found it dry. Where was Elswyth? He'd a mind to take a jug of mead, and her, to his chamber.

"Only this..."

Eldberg glared, then sighed. "Very well, Sigrid, speak and be done —but then no more."

"Watch her well, my Jarl, for she's one to use her wiles to trap a man. There's something of the witch in her. You must have noticed she looks like..." Her hand came again to his arm. "Perhaps 'tis I who am foolish, but it would be the way of a sorceress to make her appearance familiar to you and worm her way beneath your skin." Sigrid's voice quavered. "I wish not to quarrel—only to show my concern."

"Your words are riddles to me, Sigrid." Eldberg rubbed his forehead. "But we'll have no more dispute. Let this be an end to it."

He looked over at her—his little enchantress—standing at the far end of the hall, beside Sigrid's chamber. She held her hand to her brow, looking weary. There was a resigned despondency to her.

Perhaps he'd worked her too hard in his bed.

I can do with her just as I like. She's my captive. My thrall. My revenge.

But she was something else, too.

There was an element of truth in Sigrid's warning, for wasn't this a spell of sorts—when a man couldn't take his eyes from a woman?

She was bending to fill Sweyn's cup, her long hair loose-plaited and golden, falling over her shoulder.

Eldberg's attention flickered to the commander of his battle-guard. He'd grasped the end of Elswyth's plait and was drawing her downward, whispering in her ear. Some lewd comment, most likely, for she reddened and pulled away.

The thralls of Eldberg's household were there for the taking, if his sworn-men had lust to abate. He'd never denied them that privilege, though most had their own slaves, and a wife besides.

But Elswyth was not like the others; she was for his bed alone.

He'd have words with Sweyn. No one was to touch her. He would show his blade to any cur that disobeyed him. He'd make himself clear and wipe away that covetous leer.

Eldberg had taken but five steps when he heard Thoryn's shout from the other side of the hall. "Thirka!"

There was a commotion as the thrall's platter hit the floor, showering food. Her skirts were alight. She screamed, running back and forth, beating the flames with her hands.

Eldberg leapt forward, sending her to the ground, rolling her back and forth.

"Use this!" Elswyth tossed a bundle of cloth at his feet.

With the flames smothered, Thirka's terrified cries subsided to sobs. Moaning, she looked up with wide eyes. Thoryn had bounded over the table. Kneeling at her side, he took Thirka's hand. His face was grey. "She came too close to the fire pit."

"So tired." Thirka was mumbling. "Just need to lie down."

"'Tis all right," Thoryn whispered. "I'll care for you."

He picked her up. "By your leave, Jarl, I'll take her to my hut."

How did I miss that? thought Eldberg. Thoryn was in love with the girl. Under his own nose, and he'd not realized.

"I can make a salve for the burns." Elswyth was beside them, lifting the hem of Thirka's skirt. She winced at what she saw.

"We have honey," said Ragerta. She wrung her hands. "And there's marigold in the herb garden."

"Gather them quickly, and comfrey if you have it." Elswyth paused. "If you have valerian root, we'll steep that for her to drink, and mash the others for a salve."

She turned to Thoryn. "You must spread it thickly on her feet and calves—on her hands, too. Lay Thirka down and bare her legs. You'll need some linens to wrap her, after you've applied the salve."

Eldberg beheld Elswyth in wonder. Gone were the downcast eyes and her forlorn look. A spark had lit within her, giving her new purpose.

Thoryn swallowed. "Good lady, my thanks, but—"

He looked at Eldberg. "I would have her help. I don't know if I can —" Thoryn's voice wavered.

He touched his forehead to Thirka's. "She is burnt."

Burnt.

Eldberg knew what it was to be touched by fire. The healers had made his salves, with herbs not just from Skálavík but those traded from far lands. Aloe, wasn't it, that they'd smeared over him. Cooling, soothing aloe. A small pot remained, which he yet used upon his eye.

"Sigrid!"

She hadn't moved from her place at the high table.

"The salve for my eye. Fetch it."

Cutting a segment from her apple, she took it between her teeth. "It's costly, and there will be no more until the merchant returns. Are you sure, my Jarl, that you wish to use it on this thrall?"

Eldberg clenched his fists. "Fetch it, Sigrid."

He looked from his friend to Elswyth. "Go, Thoryn, and take her with you. Ragerta will bring what you need. There's enough moon for her to see by. She'll find the plants and carry all to your hut."

Elswyth hesitated, as if disbelieving, then hurried after Thoryn.

Only after they'd left did Sigrid come storming over to him, her face twisted in rage.

"That bitch! She dared enter my chamber and took it! My new cape!"

It was a rare thing for Eldberg to laugh, but he felt it rise in him now. The cloth in which they'd wrapped Thirka had been the same red as Elswyth's dress.

12

ELSWYTH

August 4th, 960AD

Thirka had been fortunate, Eldberg's quick-thinking had saved her from greater injury. She'd heal if her wounds were kept clean. There would be scarring, but she'd walk again. The burns on her hands were superficial; her palms were already accustomed to working close to the fire's heat.

Ragerta and I had worked quickly to prepare the unguent of honey, comfrey and marigold, spreading it thickly, then wrapping with strips of linen. We used the aloe where the burns seemed most severe: the back of Thirka's knees and her lower thigh. To ease her discomfort, we mashed valerian root, steeping in hot water. This, she was to sip every waking hour. I'd find willow bark when there was more time, for that was the best remedy in subduing pain, and it was easy to chew. Perhaps the forest held witch hazel, too. Once Thirka began to heal, it would aid the process.

"You have my thanks." Thoryn clasped us both by the hand as we reached the longhouse. "If I can repay you, then let me know the manner, and it shall be done."

The night sky was already lightening, the fjord shimmering gold beneath the rising sun. A breeze was blowing in from the sea, and all was hushed. The residents of Skálavík were sleeping, although there was movement in the harbor. The fishermen were early to rise, pushing out beneath those violet-shadowed mountains.

We all needed rest, but the early morning light was too beautiful to turn from, and I had no eagerness to join the one who awaited me. Ragerta and I stood, watching as Thoryn retreated.

"His mother died early in the spring. He'd been living alone," said Ragerta sadly.

"He has no thrall?" I'd noticed a woman's touch in the woven coverings for his bed and walls, but the cauldron had been empty, and his tunic looked to have gone many days without being washed.

Ragerta gave a small smile. "He sold her. Thirka says he's promised not to have another woman in the house until she can join him."

"Well, she's under his roof, now." I gave Ragerta a nudge. "Perhaps that's where she'll stay."

"If the jarl permits it." She yawned. "A strange night it was, and I'd say the gods had a hand in it. Many are the stories of lovers united after sore trials. Thirka's accident may bring them together."

Aye, if the Beast has a heart and will let her go.

I'd seen little of it until now, but nor had I expected him to act as he had, risking himself for one so insignificant in his eyes.

The two sentries walking the perimeter of the longhouse had made their circuit and paused before us now.

"Best get to bed," said one. "The mistress will be shaking you out of it afore the cock crows twice."

"Unless you'd prefer to tarry with us?" The other gave a wink. "We'll lie you down all right, but I can't swear you'll get any sleep."

"An attractive offer, I'm sure." Ragerta rolled her eyes. "But I'll take my own finger over a poke from you. 'Twill be cleaner, at any rate!"

The guards laughed and gave Ragerta's rump a friendly smack as we turned to go in.

Fleetingly, I wondered if I might have run in those moments that we'd been alone. Ragerta wouldn't have stopped me.

Don't be ridiculous. You wouldn't have made it to the trees.

But my time will come.

Better to be patient.

Watch and learn; discover the best way.

I'll have only one chance.

Inside the hall, Kellick, the lad who chopped wood and ran other errands, had stacked the trenchers and cups to one side, but they'd not been washed. That job might fall to me, besides many others now that Thirka was unable to help. Sigrid was happy to work her loom, but I didn't imagine she took the dirty work of the household.

Though I was weary, the prospect pleased me. The more I was needed for other tasks, the less time I might spend in Eldberg's bed, and the more I'd learn about this place I'd come to.

I paused at the curtain. Was he awake? The bed creaked, and I heard a sigh and a grunting snore. Would he even know if I didn't join him? I could sleep on a bench in the hall—like the other thralls. But, he would know when he woke, and it served me in no way to stir his anger.

Wearing my shift, I took my place beside him.

He sighed again and turned, his arm coming over me.

I stiffened at his touch, but he was still asleep, and dreaming—of something that disturbed him, it seemed, for he cried out, though not loud enough to wake himself.

He tossed and mumbled, then curled back to me once more. I lay listening, as his murmurs became words I understood: "No" and "Find her".

He pulled me tighter to the curve of his body, and his lips found my neck.

"My love, my love…"

With his caress, he repeated the name of the woman he dreamed of.

Bretta.

In the weeks that followed, Thoryn came to the longhouse each morning, escorting me to his home to attend Thirka. In his care, she flourished, healing more quickly than I'd expected.

He'd offered Eldberg twice her value, and they were to wed as soon as Thirka could stand unaided.

The jarl did not speak of it, merely purchasing two thralls to replace her: a married couple of Norse blood and older years, enslaved during a raid to the north. Though Sigrid kept us busy, the work became easier, with more shoulders to bear the burden.

Eldberg's moods were varied: at times angry, at others, considerate. There were days when he kept me in his bed, watching as he caused my tension to build. He would edge me toward release, making me shudder with passion I could not withhold.

I tried to close my mind against all that shamed me, telling myself that a thrall lacked the privilege of choice. I wanted to defy him, yet a strange intimacy grew between us. It was as if two men resided within him.

Despite these thoughts, I didn't forget that I was his captive, and he my master—for as long as it amused him. When that time was over, I knew not what would come. He could dispose of me in whatever fashion he saw fit. Perhaps he'd sell me in some far-off market, to whoever paid the best price; he'd sell my child, too, if it lived.

The need to escape remained with me. To stow away on some trading vessel would likely take me from one danger to another. To attempt a crossing of the mountains would be madness. The best plan seemed to be to follow the river which had brought me to Skálavík. That path, I knew, would return me to Svolvaen, although I had no idea of what remained there.

If my old friends had survived, did they think me dead, or that I'd colluded with Skálavík to bring about the events of that terrible night? It pained me to think of it. The friendships I'd made had been precious to me—hard won as they were.

Astrid. Ylva. Torhilde. Helka... And Eirik. Was it foolish of me to hope they might still live? Hadn't I seen the longhouse set afire and heard the screams of those within? Hadn't I witnessed Eldberg stand over Eirik and plunge a blade into his body?

I oft saw Eirik in my dreams, so vividly—his shoulders squared for battle, his sword raised in defiance.

If Svolvaen was no more, reaching Bjorgen would be my best chance. Jarl Ósvífur would grant me protection, surely, honoring my position as Eirik's widow. Perhaps, Helka and Leif had survived the attack, and I'd find them safe there, although it hardly seemed possible to hope. If they were alive, wouldn't they have come and bargained for my release?

Still, I needed to believe there was a place for me, somewhere beyond Skálavík.

Wormwood for stomach cramps, milfoil to stop bleeding, burdock to ease aches in the bones, and feverfew to subdue a headache. I touched each plant as I recounted them to myself, then broke off a stem of lavender: mugwort, chicory, chamomile, angelica, yarrow, and plantain.

I'd grown the same plants in Svolvaen, using them in so many combinations when I'd been seeking a cure for the disease that plagued us. Little had I known, then, that the answer lay in the caves of the fjord, where a particular seaweed grew thick on the walls.

The herb garden had been Bretta's and had grown neglected, nettles growing through the rows of plants. Not that nettle leaves weren't useful, but they couldn't be allowed to swamp everything around them.

Sigrid shouldn't have allowed it to become overgrown, but it wasn't my place to correct her. Instead, I resolved to tidy it a little each day.

This morning, I was looking for fennel and thyme. With comfrey and marigold, they'd make a good salve for Eldberg's eye, which still wept and seemed unwilling to heal.

Beyond the little garden, where the grass grew long, I spotted the frothy white flowers of giant cow parsley. Now there was a source of retribution! A drop of sap from its stem would burn his vision entirely. However, it struck me that I would never, now, want to inflict such a thing upon him.

With passing time, the urge to take my vengeance had faded. I might easily have concealed a knife and slit his throat as he slept, but I'd lost the taste for such an act.

When I fled, I vowed, it would be without blood upon my hands.

Still, I jumped at the feel of Eldberg's touch upon my shoulder.

"Mixing your potions, thrall?" He plucked the thyme from my fingers, raising it to his nose.

"For you, my Jarl." I held out all I'd gathered. "You've allowed me to help Thirka; I'll help you, too, if you'll permit it."

"You find my injury unappealing?" The old hardness was in his voice. "I'm not handsome enough for you?" He grabbed me by the shoulders. "'Tis easily remedied, for I may have my fill of you without either of us seeing the other's face."

"Nay. You're too easily offended. I thought only to ease the discomfort of this wound that's so long in healing."

He let go, and a shadow passed over his features—a fleeting glimpse of remorse, I thought, for his having spoken harshly.

It was not his way to take back words spoken or to apologize but he drew me to his chest. "I came to find you on an errand of my own, and it shall serve both purposes, if you wish to attempt the curing of me. The merchant who sold us the aloe some months ago has returned, and his ship carries other remedies. It would be well to create a chest of medicines. Thoryn tells me of your skill. You should help me choose, for I trust your judgement as well as any healer in Skálavík."

It was a great compliment—the first I'd heard from his lips, but I knew better than to appear too pleased, or to set any store by it.

Rather, I tilted back my head, offering my lips, which he took with eagerness, bold and demanding. He wrapped me within his arms as he claimed my mouth thoroughly. It was enough, that kiss, to rouse his manhood and, when he broke off, he was breathing heavily. Shrugging off his tunic, he lay it flat upon the chamomile in which we stood and guided me to lay upon it.

"You cannot mean... not here!" I protested, but he had already loosened the fastening of his trousers.

"It's my wish. As for your modesty, worry not, for the plants grow tall enough to conceal us."

There was no arguing thereafter, for he claimed another kiss and moved between my legs.

It was with some lightness of heart that I walked by Eldberg's side to the harbor. I'd never been permitted farther than Thoryn's hut—and only then in his company. At other times, I'd been under the watchful eye of Sigrid or the longhouse guard.

Like Svolvaen, Skálavík's heart lay in its harbor—but it was more than a place of fishing. As we descended the headland, Eldberg told me that merchants often visited, trading for Skálavík's whalebone and whale oil, hides and herring, axes and arrow heads, and blades of all description. The forge was worked by six strong men, whose skill attracted many in pursuit of fine weapons. The metal ore came from the very rock above the settlement.

In return, Skálavík purchased amber beads from the Baltic lands, soapstone, salt, silks and other fine cloth, and grain. The land here did not lend itself to the growing of such crops, and much barley was needed for bread and ale.

The place bustled with people jostling to peruse the many goods on sale. The scent of cook-fires mingled with the pungent odors of fish and livestock, while buyers haggled noisily. We made our way past stalls of nuts and cheeses, the marketgoers parting as Eldberg approached. They eyed me with curiosity which was in no manner concealed. I'd picked out the chamomile from my hair and smoothed myself as best I could, but I felt the shabbiness of my appearance. The dress I wore had been on my back near three weeks without washing, since I'd no other to replace it.

Our destination was a ship anchored in the bay, from which a small rowboat had been sent. It waited for us at the pier's end. Eldberg jumped straight in and held his hand to help me board.

"This captain prefers to remain on the water with his cargo—it being of particular value." He nodded at the man standing on deck, watching our approach. "It suits me well enough, since it offers more privacy for our transactions."

A rope ladder was cast down the side, enabling us to climb up, hand over hand.

I was surprised at once by the size of the vessel and its orderliness. The deck was broad and mostly clear but for neatly looped coils of rope. The sails had been well-tied, enabling the ship to sit perfectly still at anchor.

"*Selamlar,* Yusuf." Eldberg inclined his head slightly before touching his forehead and heart.

"*Barış seninle olsun, arkadaşım,*" the man replied, offering the same gesture of welcome in return.

The captain smiled, his gaze flicking over me before returning to Eldberg. Behind him stood eight of his crew, each as nut-brown as their captain, with legs planted firmly and their eyes upon us. Though they appeared at ease, each wore a weapon at his belt.

"And peace be with you, my friend." Eldberg moved to clasp the other's hand.

"You have something special to trade today, yes? A treasure with eyes like jewels and skin of ivory."

A cold wave broke through me, hearing those words spoken haltingly in the Norse tongue. I looked fearfully to Eldberg. Was this the moment when he would fulfil his threat? If so, then there was no greater fool than I, for I'd begun to believe he'd be sorry to lose me, when the day came that I made my escape.

"Ha!" Eldberg answered with clear amusement, the corner of his mouth twitching. "She is mine to sell, but were I able to part with her, I'd ask for sapphires large enough to match those eyes, Yusuf."

"Forgive me." The captain dipped his head. "I merely assumed..."

Eldberg's grand reply was almost as disconcerting as my belief that he might sell me. He spoke, truly, as if I were precious to him.

"In this case, I have silks and bracelets of gold, carried from Constantinople. It is these you come for, yes, to adorn this cherished plaything and make her fit for your harem?"

"You change not a whit, Yusuf!" barked Eldberg, clearly enjoying this game, though my own temper rankled to hear them speak of me thus.

"You may tempt me with your trinkets later, though I warrant you have nothing to offer that can compare to the enticement of her bare skin. She needs no fine garments to make herself beautiful to me. I'd keep her naked all day and night, were it not that I must drag myself to attend other matters occasionally." Eldberg met my eyes, and his own were laughing still, caring not that anger flashed in mine.

"But, of course, a woman's natural state is always most desirable," came the reply.

I saw a hint of lasciviousness as the captain looked upon me again, no doubt imagining me without the cover of my gown.

Eldberg cleared his throat and composed himself, asking more seriously, "It is medicines I come for. Like those you traded before, when I was unable to greet you, and Thoryn came in my stead."

He turned his face, indicating the burns that had healed. "The aloe was effective, and we would purchase more, together with samples of other ingredients you recommend. If they prove potent, we shall buy greater volumes next time you sail to us."

"I see you are not just fortunate in your company but wise, Jarl Eldberg." The captain touched his heart. "And it will be my pleasure to supply all you require."

Turning, he uttered instructions in his own tongue, sending two of his men below deck. They returned with a chest.

Opening it, Yusuf brought forth a ceramic pot sealed with wax. "One silver piece for an amphora of aloe, my friend. For the rest, I shall prepare a small vial of each from my personal store and explain their properties. For this, in good faith, I make no charge, but shall return with the spring tides and greater volumes—from which you may purchase as much as you wish. If it pleases you, I shall trade for the furs you harvest this winter. Your foxes are particularly fine, and I have buyers who await them back in the east."

Eldberg gave his agreement, and they proceeded about the business. Yusuf decanted small quantities of colorful powders, giving their name and application: turmeric and ginger—to counteract soreness in the body and aid digestion; clove oil for relief of tooth pain; and cinnamon to ease breathing. There were twenty or more, each with its own remedy, which I committed to memory.

"And this, my friend, I'm sure you have no use for." The captain shook a small ball, making it rattle. "It increases a man's ability and sustains his force, for the creation of many children." He gave a small smile. "Though you need it not, I shall place this nutmeg with your other medicines, in case one of the men under your command wishes to test its potency."

Shaking hands, Eldberg thanked him for his thoroughness.

"What else do you have for me then, Yusuf? Show me your best. Something fit to be worn by my golden queen."

I reddened to hear him call me such, for the jest was at my expense. Whatever he named me, I was still his slave, without any right to refuse him or his gift.

The captain considered a moment before giving instruction again, sending another of his men to fetch what he requested. There were three bolts of fabric, each of sufficient length to make a gown. The first was of rich green brocade, the next in pale gold, threaded through with silver, and the last a silk of shimmering blue, its hues like those of the fjord. In addition, he produced an arm circlet intricately shaped in silver and studded with pearls. There were brooches to match.

I was speechless, for not even the fabric of my own wedding gown had been so fine, and I'd never worn any adornment of value—other than the ivory brooch given to me by Asta.

Eldberg nodded. There was a brief exchange regarding the price, but the jarl seemed little bothered about haggling. Readily, he counted a generous number of coins from his pouch. "You have a good eye.

Pack everything, and we'll leave you. I wish you a safe journey and shall look for your return."

"*Veda arkadaşım.* Farewell, my friend."

As we rowed back to the pier, Eldberg leaned forward, resting his forearms upon his knees. "You will look most elegant, my Elswyth, but I meant what I said."

"And what was that, my Jarl?" I looked over the water, not trusting myself to meet the intensity of his gaze.

"No matter how fine your gown, I shall always prefer you out of it."

13

ELDBERG

October 31st, 960AD

The skuas, gulls, and terns had flown, leaving the wind to moan its loss through the crags that hung above Skálavík.

The time had come to mark the rite of *Alfablót,* to honor the souls of the dead and the spirits of the dark—the *Dökkalfar.* Unseen by the living, mysterious, and at their most powerful during the long nights, such forces dwelled in the mountain above Skálavík. Tonight, they would receive their sacrifice, and all men would remember their frailty in the darkness of the unknown.

Her face was still vivid in Eldberg's memory.

He looked to the rolling, rippling pulse of light in the northern sky and, in his mind, he reached for her.

Do you see me, Bretta?

Sweyn led the young bull within the sacred circle—a stone for each man of Skálavík, and each man behind a stone.

"We call upon our male ancestors to protect us—to speak for us among the dark ones." Eldberg's voice rang out, addressing all surrounding him. "We offer this *blót,* this libation, and we beseech mercy through the winter's long cold, that we may live to see the sun return."

Raising his axe, Eldberg swung it thrice about his head before burying it with a splitting thud in the calf's skull. It was a clean kill, the creature falling to the ground with the blade still lodged in the bone. It gave no bellow—only a sudden jerking and a wide-eyed stare.

Planting his foot firmly against the calf's shoulder, Eldberg released the weapon and gestured to Sweyn. Kneeling, Sweyn held a shallow bowl beside the creature's neck. One plunge of the dagger brought forth a gush of blood.

When the vessel was full, he raised it up and Eldberg dipped his thumb into the liquid. He marked the forehead of his commander and then his own. While the bull's life-force soaked the ground beneath their feet, Eldberg brought the dish to his lips and drank.

"Pledged in loyalty, we stand, brother to brother, until we enter that other realm."

"Until we enter that other realm." The response travelled the circle with the passing of the bowl, all drinking and receiving his jarl's mark.

Having completed its journey, the dish returned to the center of the circle, and each man nodded soberly to his neighbor. There would be revelry later, with the animal's meat roasted and a portion brought back to this place with a tankard of mead. For now, they would depart in silence, carrying the carcass of the beast between them.

The wind was rising, and Eldberg could smell storm clouds gathering.

"I would speak with you, my Jarl." Sweyn drew him aside. "There is more for us to fear than the forces of the hidden world."

Eldberg surveyed his commander. "You wish to warn me, Sweyn?"

The other squared his shoulders. "That wench; she has bewitched you." He wetted his lips. "And the rounder her belly grows, the more she has you under her spell."

"You're brave, this night, Sweyn." Eldberg fixed him with a hard stare. "You think to tell me whether this thrall deserves the warmth of my bed?"

Sweyn's glance darted away. "She rules not only your bed. The clothes she wears are finer than Sigrid's, and she no longer performs the duties of a thrall. There are two mistresses now, for the other slaves follow her more willingly than their true lady."

"If 'tis true, then it speaks more of Sigrid's lack than Elswyth's. As to her duties, they are mine to decide."

"Forgive me." Sweyn raised his gaze. "But the men are saying you let this woman—an enemy of Skálavík—twist you to her bidding. You neglect your visits to the harbor and the mines."

He swallowed hard. "Give her to the men of the guard and you'll be free again."

Eldberg tasted ashes on his tongue. No man had the right to speak to him thus. No man should dare. He closed his hand around Sweyn's neck.

"You think to judge me?" Eldberg squeezed harder. "You go too far." Slowly, he raised the man in his grip, lifting his feet from the ground. "She has soothed the disquiet of my grief, and her skills have brought healing to my eye. For that I favor her, but I am her master."

"Your eye, my lord!" He spluttered, kicking his feet. "She sent Thoryn deep into the caves of the fjord, making him bring back every seaweed he could find. There was one she wanted. 'Tis that she used in the poultice—a type that grows only in the dark, hidden." Sweyn gasped for air. "Her spells use not the medicines you purchased from the Mikklagard Turk. She's no better than the old woman who lives in the mountain, dabbling in things no man should know."

Eldberg let Sweyn drop, his lip curling in distaste. "You're relieved of your post as commander of the guard. From tomorrow, you'll report to the mine."

"That place! No!" Sweyn crawled back, clutching at his throat. He looked up at Eldberg, his mouth slack, disbelieving. "I've served you faithfully. I've done all you bid." He shook his head. "I don't deserve this."

"You've served yourself." Eldberg touched the hilt of the dagger sheathed at his waist. "I release you from your bond. Go where you will. If the mine doesn't suit you, find your fortune elsewhere."

Sweyn scrambled to his feet, eyes dark with hatred. He went for the blade at his own belt, but Eldberg was too quick. His weapon slashed the back of Sweyn's wrist before he could draw.

Sweyn cried out, clutching the wound beneath his arm.

"I have your answer." Eldberg wiped clean the blood from his dagger. "Know that I let you live only in token of your past service. Tomorrow, you'll leave. I care not where you go. If I see you again, my blade will open your throat."

Sweyn spat on the ground. "Curse you to the mouth of Hel, and that bitch!"

Eldberg took a single step forward.

It was enough.

Sweyn ran—down the headland and away.

Rain was falling. He ought to get inside and join his men, but a stronger desire was calling to him, beneath the shadow of the mountain.

He wanted to see the wise woman, Hildr. It was an auspicious night—*Alfablót*. The night of the dead.

What better time to consult those unseen forces? To seek out the seer who existed between the dark souls of the mountain and the world of men.

He'd only once visited her cave. When Beornwold had first taken Eldberg as his commander, offering him a permanent home, he'd insisted on Hildr casting the runes.

She'd spoken in riddles, of course. He'd been impatient, wanting to know what she beheld. Those white-shaded eyes had unnerved him; blind, yet seeing something others could not. She'd touched his left side, then pulled her hand away. Too hot, she'd said. Then, covering his eye with her palm, had mumbled something about Odin's mark.

It had seemed nonsense at the time.

He knew better now.

Eldberg pulled his wolfskin closer and turned his face to the mountain.

His memory hadn't failed him. Though the entrance was overhung with vines, the patch of ground in front bore evidence of feet: those of the crone and those who visited her.

There was a flapping of wings and an owl swooped low, coming to rest in the tree to one side of the entrance. It turned its slow-blinking gaze upon him.

Inside, the cave was as he remembered it; twigs and stones sat in piles, runes were scratched into the walls. There were bundled blankets, a cooking pot, knives, and an axe.

The scent of her fire—pine branches and moss—was strong. The place was cold, despite the well-stoked flames. Smoke curled upward, drawn through a crevice in the upper rock. Water dripped somewhere in the back.

Hildr lifted her head, sniffing the air, her clouded eyes turned in his direction. She was more bone than flesh; sinew wrapped in rags.

"I've been waiting for you." She gestured with her hand. "Sit. Drink with me." There were two cups.

Eldberg brought his nose cautiously to the brew; fungi and twigs. He grimaced and heard her chuckle.

"Nothing to poison you—only to help." She sipped from her own cup. "You'll live long yet, but you've not come to ask that, have you?"

"Nay." Eldberg took some of the liquid into his mouth, making himself hold it there, ignoring the bitterness.

The runes were laid out beside her: fragments of bone—some carved, beaks and claws, an owl's feather. She touched them lightly with her fingertips. "But you have a question."

"Perhaps."

"Then tell it to the dark ones." Her voice, previously as frail as a moth's wing, was insistent. She reached for him, taking his hand, placing it within the runes. "Picture all in your mind. They will hear."

He enclosed the fragments between his two palms, rattling them as he'd done the first time, then tossing all upon the ground. They scattered, falling randomly. He peered, looking for some pattern, but there was none. Nevertheless, the seer bent forward, her fingers trembling over the pieces, feeling for where each had settled.

"Yes," her voice crooned. "I saw it even before you came."

"What?" Eldberg had to stop himself from shaking her. "What do you see?"

"Two claws are touching. There is conflict: in your past, in these days you are living, and more to come. The beak is upward—sharp, dangerous, the threat of wounding. Life hangs in the balance. Someone wishes ill upon you. There is envy. There is betrayal."

Eldberg hissed. "This I know without you telling me. What else, old woman?"

Revealing more gum than tooth, Hildr smiled. "What you desire will not bring you happiness."

Eldberg closed his eyes, suddenly weary. His journey had been wasted. She'd told him nothing of value.

"You do not wish to hear, but you must learn." Carefully, she gathered up the runes, placing them as they had been, each in their allotted place. "You are the spider in the web and the fly. Each movement determines what will come. Much is written, but there are many paths. You must choose."

Eldberg sighed. He'd heard enough.

Only as he stood, did she crawl forward. Her fingers hooked through the crossed laces that held the fur about his leg.

"Leave the dead to rest." Her voice rasped. "And look to the living."

Her head jerked up, her eyes staring beyond him.

"In the forest! Find her!"

14

SWEYN

October 31ˢᵗ, 960AD

The hall was full. People lounged on the long benches, joking, and laughing. An arm-wrestling contest had begun at the central tables. Slabs of beef were already searing on the roasting griddles, the calf having been promptly butchered. The rich scent of stew carried over the fire's smoke.

Sweyn sidled up to where the wench was supervising the opening of a new barrel of mead. He tugged on her sleeve. "The jarl has asked for you. He's waiting."

She seemed not to hear him above the merriment around them, so he jerked his head, mouthing the word clearly. "Outside."

Elswyth frowned. "Isn't he coming? They're all waiting for him."

Sweyn glanced about. As far as he could see, no one was waiting for anything—except more mead.

"You're to come with me." Sweyn placed his hand under her elbow, guiding her from the barrel.

Warily, she let him lead her onward.

Across the room, Sigrid caught his eye and glowered. She'd

become sourer by the day, displaced and disgruntled. Before Sweyn had gotten Elswyth to the door, Sigrid had intercepted them.

"She has things to do here. We all have. Where's she going?" Sigrid barked her question, grasping Elswyth by the other arm.

"Jarl's orders." Sweyn shrugged. "She's to join him on the head-land. Some part of the ritual he wants her to take part in—favored as she is." He gave a sickly smile, knowing the request would rile Sigrid.

"More of the same! And when we need all the help!" Sigrid spat her retort. "Go on then." She squeezed the girl's elbow sufficiently to make her wince. "Perhaps it's your blood he wants, my dear—a more powerful *blót* for the dark ones."

"Nothing like that, I'm sure." Sweyn cursed Sigrid for her cruel tongue. He'd seen the jarl striding into the trees rather than following him down, but he didn't know how long it would be until Eldberg joined them. If his plan were to work, Sweyn needed Elswyth to come quickly.

"I'm hardly dressed…" She indicated her gown—a flimsy thing of bright blue silk, worn over a simple shift of white. It was better suited to the summer months gone, but it grew hot in the hall when so many came together. The men would have their chests bare before the night was out.

"We'll not be long." Sweyn tugged her again. "Don't keep him waiting."

Sigrid gave a final scowl as he bustled Elswyth outside.

Spits of rain were now falling. The guard of two passed on their perimeter walk, shoulders hunched against the wind.

Sweyn called them over. "You're to go in and get yourselves a cup of mead. The jarl bids you well. Come out as soon as you've drunk it, mind!"

They didn't need to be told twice.

Sweyn breathed easier. He just needed to get her to the treeline, and they'd be out of sight.

"My cloak!" Elswyth tried to pull back. "I'll fetch it."

Sweyn cursed again. "Nay. 'Tis not cold enough for that—and the thing is scorched. 'Twould shame you to wear it for what the jarl has in mind."

She seemed to consider. Thoryn had returned the cape in the days after Thirka's accident. Sigrid had turned up her nose, since the inside was blackened.

Eldberg had promised Sigrid a new cape of fur once the hunting season began, and the same for Elswyth—to Sigrid's disgust.

Sweyn could see the girl thinking. She'd been wearing it the night Sweyn had abducted her. She seemed suddenly aware of how tightly he held her arm; of how persistently he was dragging her farther from the door.

"Stop! I don't want to go. This isn't right. I don't believe you!"

In a single motion, Sweyn struck her forehead with his own. She crumpled immediately. With a last look about him, he hefted her onto his shoulder. Even with her rounded belly, she was an easy weight to lift.

He skirted the edge of the longhouse and made for the forest's edge.

Sweyn carried her as deeply into the trees as he dared. Too close and they'd be spotted; too far, and he'd waste precious time.

By Fenrir's teeth, he hated that berserker scum. He should've died in the fire, and everything would have worked out differently. Sweyn had kept things running while that ungrateful bastard had lain at death's door. Who else but him would have become jarl in Eldberg's stead? Even that miserable bitch Sigrid would have given her blessing.

Now, if he wanted to keep his head on his neck, he'd have to leave. Eldberg had recovered from injuries that would've killed an ordinary man, and he remained the strongest among them. No one could stand against him in single combat and expect to win.

But he'd give Eldberg something to remember him by—and he'd be back all right. No one treated Sweyn like this and got away with it.

As for this one!

Sweyn knelt over Elswyth, gripping her face with one hand. She was coming round slowly, not fully conscious yet.

Bringing her to Skálavík had been a mistake.

It was true she'd distracted Eldberg in those first weeks—an unexpected boon, all things considered—but her influence had changed him in ways Sweyn couldn't have predicted.

Eldberg was known for his savage temper, coupled with warrior strength and skill with the sword. Yet, during his marriage to Bretta, he'd starting using his head as ably as his fighting arm.

Skálavík would thrive as a trading port. His legacy, Eldberg had called it; for them to one day rival Hedeby as a place for merchants to gather. Wealth would flow into Skálavík through commerce.

Bretta's death, and that of Eldberg's unborn child, had near broken the jarl, his grief reducing him to the barbarian he'd been all those years ago. Sweyn had rubbed his hands gleefully to see it, for it eased the path to his own ambitions.

However, these months past, Elswyth had soothed the savage beast, taming him once more. It had stirred much talk—and not in criticism of the Svolvaen whore. Far from neglecting his duties as jarl, Eldberg had embraced them with greater vigor. He'd expanded the output of the mine and the number of men trained in the forging of weapons. Meanwhile, his harbor guard ensured the smooth running of the market and the safety of all vessels entering Skálavík's fjord.

Even if Eldberg hadn't realized it himself, Sweyn could see what was coming. The jarl would free Elswyth as he had Thirka; once she'd delivered her child—perhaps sooner. Then he'd marry the wench and sire his own heir.

Sweyn's ambitions for himself had been thwarted, but there was one part of Eldberg's future Sweyn could ruin. With any luck, the discovery would send their jarl hurtling back to the chasm from which he'd climbed.

Elswyth's lids flickered as Sweyn took hold of her neck. He'd crush her throat quick and easy, and then he'd be gone.

But, looking down at her, he was reminded of why he'd taken her in the first place. The flimsy gown she was wearing had gotten damp from the rain. It clung to her breasts—even more voluptuous in her ripe condition. The cool air had tightened her nipples. He dropped one hand to squeeze her flesh. Between finger and thumb, he pinched the peak, and she whimpered, though did not fully stir.

It was enough to send a jolt of heat to his groin.

By Thor and Odin and all the gods, this one wanted Skálavík cock and, before he broke her pretty neck, he'd give it to her.

Hungrily, he brought up her skirts, shoving her legs apart with his knee.

She was a captured slave, and he'd fuck her like one.

Grasping her hips, he delved his fingers into her sheath. She was ready enough for the piercing. There would be nothing to stop him entering to the hilt.

Her hair fanned loose about her head—golden silk upon the half-rotten leaves and moss. Her lips, full and soft, invited him. Everything that Eldberg had enjoyed would be his.

He bore down upon her, plundering her mouth while his arousal nudged her wetness.

Too late did he realize his folly.

As her teeth clamped down on his tongue, Sweyn's mouth filled with blood.

Elswyth

I roused to pain in my forehead, to an inability to breathe, to the heaviness of him upon me. Instinct made me bite the probing thing in my mouth, and his bellow broke through to awaken me.

He sprung up, cursing, and the lifting of his weight enabled me to scrabble away from him.

Sweyn!

Gulping, I screamed, but he was upon me immediately. A hard slap sent me sprawling into the leaves. He leapt upon me then, holding both my arms tight to the ground.

"Do that again, and I'll snap your neck."

Through eyes filled with tears, I saw the fury in his. Breathless, I forced out my words. "Harm me, and Eldberg will kill you for it."

"I'll be long-gone." His snarl was that of a wild creature.

"And when they find my body? Eldberg will know it was you, Sweyn."

"He might." A wicked gleam lit his eye. "Or the beasts will make short work of you, and there'll be no evidence. He'll think you ran away."

I gulped back my fear.

It was true. It's what they all would think.

I had to keep him talking. Eldberg might be out here. He might have heard me scream. I just needed time.

"What have I done, Sweyn?" I spoke softly. "Why do you hate me?"

"You?" Sweyn hurled the word back at me. "It's him I want to hurt!"

I didn't understand. My head was throbbing. Had I hit it when I fell? Nothing made sense. Sweyn had authority, status, and respect. Why was he doing this?

I made my voice calm. "You won't harm me, Sweyn. You know it's not right. You'll be killing the baby as well as me. What do the gods say about that? What do the ancestors say? Aren't they close tonight? Aren't they watching?"

"Shut up!" Sweyn leaned on my arms more heavily, and I cried out in pain. "You know naught about it. You don't belong here. You're nothing!"

Of all the things he might have said, this cut deep.

I'd spent a lifetime not belonging.

But I wasn't nothing.

I looked into his face, summoning all my strength to speak clearly. "They tried to kill me in Svolvaen, but they couldn't. They bound me to the pier, but I escaped. I lived in the caves, and I climbed up through the cliffs. Do you believe an ordinary woman could do that? If I was nothing, do you think I'd still be alive!"

Sweyn's eyes narrowed.

He was unsure; I felt it.

Some had believed me an enchantress. I had no magic. I wove no spells. But I had other power; that of a woman who refused to be cowed. No matter what happened, I knew myself. I'd made mistakes and paid for them, but I was a survivor.

If I could make Sweyn fear me, I might yet live.

"I vow by my own god and all those that govern here, harm me and I'll curse you. Every foul pestilence I'll visit on you, until you'll wish yourself dead and that you'd never laid eyes upon me!"

He let go of my arms, leaning back.

He was afraid.

From somewhere in the bushes, there was a rustle. I doubted Sweyn would have noticed before, but his attention darted up, ears straining.

"Go quickly while you have the chance. Go, Sweyn! Leave me here to the animals of the forest if you like, but run while you can."

"You think to fool me with such nonsense?" He frowned.

Somewhere, far off, an owl hooted.

I froze as he pulled his knife from its sheath. After all I'd said, was he still going to take my life? I watched in horror as he took the blade to the hem of my gown, tearing off one long strip, then another.

The first he used to bind my ankles. The second he wound around my wrists, placed behind my back.

"If the creatures take you, it won't be my doing. You're in the hands of the gods now. Let them save you."

I feared he was right.

My fate lay in who would find me first—Eldberg or the predators who roamed this dark place.

15

ELSWYTH

October 31st, 960AD

No matter how I twisted, my fingers wouldn't reach the cloth that bound my wrists. I refused to give in. I knew not in which direction Skálavík lay, but I believed some force watched over me. I had faith in that guiding power.

Drawing my feet under, I managed to stand, but the bindings round my ankles were too tight. I lost balance, pitching forward into the damp leaves. Again I tried, and again, but succeeded only in scratching my arms and face on brambles.

How often I'd imagined escaping; had thought of which path I might take through the forest's edge and down to the meadows, finding the river and following it back to Svolvaen.

I'd wondered how I might evade detection.

Now, I needed to be found.

I needed Eldberg to come for me before wild beasts sniffed my blood.

Rolling to place my back against a tree, I sat cold and shivering. How many eyes were watching me? I listened for the breath of the forest's creatures, imagining movement where there was none.

Should I call out? If Eldberg were nearby, it would help him find me, but what of those other beasts? What if I summoned them also?

I closed my mind to what else might be lurking: entities for which I had no name. I'd brushed against the unknown things of the other-world before, when Asta's restless spirit had reached across the veil.

Curling small like a child, I buried my nose to my knees.

Time passed, the shadows grew darker, and then I was certain I heard breaking twigs.

Something was in the bushes.

I looked about. Was there a branch I might grasp to defend myself? Nothing was close. In any case, my hands were bound.

Whatever it is, let it not see me. Let it pass by.

I sat very still, breathing shallow, but my pulse galloped.

When the thing exploded from the undergrowth, I shrieked.

Wings flapped. It squawked, whirling away—a pheasant of some sort.

A sob stuck in my throat, making me laugh and cry.

Only a bird, nothing to hurt me.

But, through the gloom, something else was staring at me, no more than twenty footsteps away. Bright eyes were gleaming. I saw a flash of tusk.

A boar!

Those rough-bristled swine had vicious tempers. A single gore could tear a man in two.

"Go away!" I shouted, then again.

I growled. I hissed. I barked like a dog.

Still, the creature watched. I heard its grunt, and it emerged from the bracken. Swinging its head, it snorted, making ready to charge. It pawed the ground, throwing up leaves and chunks of moss.

I screamed, drawing back against the tree. My time had come.

But there was another sound.

A soft footstep?

The beast raised its snout, nostrils twitching, sensing some other presence. I couldn't see and hadn't the courage to turn.

A wolf? Or more than one?

Would they fight over which was to make a meal of me?

And then a steady voice, low and firm, commanded me. "Be still."

Briefly, I saw the glinting blade. Eldberg threw his axe true, driving it into the boar's neck. The creature thrashed and squealed, blood gushing. In fury, it lowered its head and rushed to meet its attacker, but Eldberg's dagger was ready. As it was almost upon him, he sank it through the boar's snout.

The boar fell immediately. It rolled to its side, pawing the air. Eldberg acted swiftly, delivering the final thrust to end the creature's pain.

I closed my eyes, not wishing to see more. I was aware of Eldberg freeing me—first my feet and then my hands. His palm was upon my forehead, then his lips. His arms came around me. Limp and numb, I gave in to exhaustion.

I wished the bed would stop tilting back and forth. Tentatively, I touched my forehead. What had happened? The events of the night seemed unreal, though my aches and bruising told me otherwise.

It had been my barking that had brought Eldberg to my exact spot. Of Sweyn there was no sign. The harbor-watch reported that he'd taken a small fishing boat and left the fjord not long ago. The vessel might carry him some way if he avoided wrecking on the coastal rocks.

Eldberg helped me out of my filthy clothing, rubbed dry my hair, and wrapped me warm in his bed. He pulled the furs to my shoulders, but still I was chilled.

Ragerta brought warm buttermilk, and he bid me drink, though slowly. He paced the chamber, then folded his arms. His voice was stern. "Promise me that you'll never leave."

I was too weary to argue, but neither did I wish to tell him a falsehood.

"You know that I did not. Sweyn took me."

He waved his hand dismissively. "Of course, since you would

hardly have devised to bind your own hands and feet. I ask because I wish you to say it."

He came to sit beside me, taking my hand. "You could have died."

It was true.

I'd prayed for Eldberg to come, and he'd done so, but I could never promise to abandon hope of my freedom.

Instead, I asked, "Why did you risk yourself for me?"

"Because you're mine—and a man protects what is his."

I hadn't the strength to tell him again that I wasn't his. I'd long ago exhausted such reasoning. An uneasy peace had fallen between us, his early brutality having spent itself, and there was much for which I was indebted.

Ragerta brought some of the aloe. Eldberg dipped into the pot and touched the soothing balm to the welts on my wrist.

"You haven't promised yet."

"I…" The words stuck in my throat. If I said it, what resistance was left?

"Elswyth." He locked me in his gaze, then leaned in, until his mouth was close to my own.

I wanted to turn away from his kiss, to close myself to him, but I couldn't. His lips were soft, coaxing me with gentle tugs and nudges. His tongue slid upon mine, and I lost myself in the desire to be caressed tenderly.

I told myself to no longer think; to set aside what I'd been before, to set aside the past. There would be only now, and the kisses of a man who was both strong and vulnerable. Weren't we the same: self-ish, cruel, hurting—yet needing to be loved? He was my enemy, and he was myself.

And yet, I was compelled to speak my mind. I broke the kiss, saying, "Give your promise—to release me from thralldom, so that my child will be born free."

"You need fear nothing."

I wished it to be true—to be sure that his feelings for me were stronger than his desire for revenge. Eldberg had destroyed everything I'd cared for. Such a thing could not be easily forgiven, but I wanted to set aside that anger. It had eaten at me for too long.

He reached for both my hands. "I wish to be whole again and take you to wife."

His expression—always so mocking—was no longer so. I'd witnessed him in every mood, but never this: so intense, so sure.

He turned my palm, bringing it to his lips. "If I enslave you, it shall be through love."

The words were enough, and I pushed down the furs, bearing myself to him. "Touch me, my lord." It was a demand but softly made.

Gently, he obeyed, trailing his fingers across my breasts, and across the fullness of my stomach, hard with the babe, until he found where I was wet.

No other command was necessary. He brought himself naked to me, and I embraced the body I'd come to know so well: the tight curve of his buttocks and powerfully muscled thighs, the firm contours of his back.

As he moved within me, the expression in his eyes stilled my breath—for it was as if he were searching for my soul, thirsty for more than the oblivion of shuddering surrender.

It was a yearning that haunted us both.

16

EIRIK

November 1st, 960AD

He became aware of voices and clattering somewhere, far off. All was dark, for he wasn't ready to open his eyes, but he stretched his fingertips, rubbing at the weave of the cloth upon which he lay.

He tried shifting a little, reaching out for Elswyth, but his arms were heavy and wouldn't obey, as if only his mind had woken and not his body.

If only he could move, he'd find her. She would be there, next to him. He wanted to kiss her—his wife; to draw her close, his fingers tangled in her golden hair.

"Elswyth." His lips moved to form the word, but his mouth was too dry to make the sound. He tried again, to no avail.

Someone squeezed his hand, and a feminine voice asked, "Are you awake?"

Of course, he was. He could hear her—Helka.

He returned the pressure of his sister's touch.

"Thank the gods!"

His hand received a sharper squeeze and was lifted to his sister's cheek. Had she been crying? What was the matter?

A man was allowed to sleep late on the day after his wedding, surely. He couldn't remember getting to bed, but it wasn't the first time another had carried him. If a man couldn't get drunk on the day he married the woman he loved, when could he?

Though his throat was parched, his head was free of the ache that usually accompanied a surfeit of mead.

"Drink this."

A cup touched his lips, wetting them, and Eirik swallowed gratefully. He wanted to open his eyes, but it was so difficult.

"What do you remember?"

Eirik fought to recall. The wedding feast, and Elswyth looking beautiful in her crimson gown, her diadem not of hammered gold but of meadow flowers. And the room hung gloriously with boughs of blooms.

Bride and groom, they'd paraded, then been carried from one end of the hall to the other, passed above the heads of their guests.

How loudly everyone had cheered.

There had been games, riddles, and wrestling, and enough meat to fill a man's belly thrice over.

Later, Elswyth, overcome by the warmth of the room, had gone to take some air—and Olaf had challenged him to a drinking contest. Ten horns they'd supped dry. "Climb on the table," Olaf had said. "Whoever reaches the end first, without falling off, will be the winner."

But he'd heard a scream. Then shouting.

Fire!

He'd looked up. The roof was crackling, amber licking between the timbers, eating the turf—dry from the good weather. Chunks were falling through.

Eirik's heart leapt in panic.

There were flames!

He squeezed Helka's hand fiercely and drew a deep breath, filling his lungs with air.

"F-fire!" He forced out the word. "Fire!" He gulped down more air. "Helka! Fire!"

He needed to waken properly and open his eyes. He needed to warn them, but it was as if a great weight were pressing him back. He fought to sit up, and a terrible pain bolted beneath his ribs.

"Shh, calm yourself." Helka's hand touched his chest. "We're all safe. The fire's out now."

She paused momentarily. "What else, Eirik? What else do you remember?"

He'd leapt down from the table. Flaming torches flew through the doorway, but still people pushed, stumbling, calling to each other, running to escape.

Helka was nearby, coughing through the smoke. Grabbing her, he'd rushed forward. They met the night air, but the hem of her gown was alight. To smother the flames, he'd pushed her to the ground.

It should have been dark, but the fire lit everything in its glow.

Where was Elswyth? Was she safe?

And then he saw. Amidst the smoke and the shouts and the rush of bodies, there were others—standing, watching. A shout of command and a glint of steel.

Instinctively, his hands reached for his sword, but there was no scabbard at his belt. Only his ceremonial dagger hung there.

He barely had time to clasp its jeweled hilt when he was pierced by pain. He saw the blade thrust clean through. Blood bubbled into his mouth. The dagger slipped from his hand. And then he was on his back, the ground strangely soft, and a figure loomed above.

Someone called his name.

The violet sky grew darker and the shouts around him faint, until there was only the ragged rattle of his breath.

The far-off voice was no more.

And the light, too, faded.

Helka

"Eirik!" Helka pinched his cheeks.

It had taken more than three phases of the moon for her brother to wake. She wouldn't allow him to slip away again so soon.

In the first days, she'd thought him lost. The injury was too severe; how could he recover? But her brother was strong. More than any other man she knew.

The Norns had woven a cruel fate for Svolvaen that night, but the blade that pierced him had only nicked his lung, penetrating beneath his ribs. He'd spilled much blood and fought a fever, but it had passed. The wound was healing well.

She'd never given up hope that he'd return to her, insisting that she tend him in her own hut. Propping him up, she'd spooned tiny amounts of broth between his lips, massaging his throat to make him swallow.

At last, one eye fluttered open.

"Elswyth." This time, he spoke her name clearly.

Helka gestured to Leif standing by the door, signaling for him to fetch the others.

Eirik needed to know. She had to tell him.

"Svolvaen was attacked. Leif escaped with others through the opening to the rear of the longhouse."

"I'm glad of it... but Elswyth?"

"We looked everywhere she might have run to, everywhere she might have hidden."

"You didn't find her?" Eirik's face was pale.

She took his hands in hers. "The two guards who'd been on watch had their throats slit." She took a deep breath. "Both had 'Skálavík' carved into their forehead."

Eirik struggled to sit up, only to fall back on the pillows. His face contorted with pain. "She's been taken—as our mother was."

"No message was received for her ransom, but I'm convinced you're right."

"We must send an emissary; ensure her safety," Eirik's voice was pleading.

"I wished to do so, but there were so many wounded. Anders volunteered, but I couldn't spare him. I needed everyone."

"All this time..." Eirik stared upward.

Neither spoke.

If Elswyth were alive, what would she have suffered? If she returned, like their mother, would she be broken in ways that could not be mended? The Beast of Skálavík had earned his name not through gentle hospitality.

"I just need a few days to get on my feet, then I'll take a boat. I'll bring her back—and if Eldberg has harmed her, he'll pay with his life."

Helka nodded. For now, she would pacify him. She and Leif had already made plans. They couldn't ignore Skálavík's act of aggression. Leif was to ride to Bjorgen and return with enough warriors to man Svolvaen's boats. They'd show Skálavík they weren't without allies.

"Elswyth is strong," Helka said what she knew Eirik needed to hear. "She'll endure."

Eirik returned his gaze to the rafters. It was too much for him to take in, Helka knew. She'd had many weeks to accept what had happened; weeks in which she and Leif had helped Svolvaen's survivors band together. The younger children, at least, had not been in the hall that night. And their attackers had ignored Svolvaen's stores, which they might so easily have razed.

"There is something else." Though Eirik looked wretched, Helka wanted him to know as much as possible. "Gunnolf sent someone to Skálavík, while we were in Bjorgen. We have a witness. He arrived only yesterday, claiming our man set alight the longhouse—upon Gunnolf's order. Many died, including Jarl Eldberg's wife."

Eirik turned to her in alarm. "Just the same..." The significance was not lost upon him.

Helka nodded. "And there was only one objective in the attack upon Svolvaen."

"Revenge." Eirik's expression was frozen. He licked at his lips, and Helka offered him water again. "Who is this witness?"

Helka turned to the door. Leif was waiting, the stranger behind him flanked by Olaf and Anders.

Helka nodded curtly. "His name is Sweyn, and he has his own score to settle."

17

ELSWYTH

December *1st*, 960AD

A s the cloak of winter fell, the mountains turned to ice and the world beneath huddled against bitter winds. The sun had retreated so far that it seemed gone forever. The long nights were upon us.

Skálavík's stores were richly laden. Eldberg and his men made many hunting trips, provisioning us with furs to be traded when the merchants returned, and with game, which we smoked and salted.

Within my belly, swollen high and round, the babe punched restless fists and feet, and I thought of how I would have placed Eirik's hand to feel its movements. It was Eldberg, instead, who watched life grow within me.

He made a cradle, finely carved and made to rock, though it would be three more moons before we held the child.

He had no wish to wait, but I needed time to put aside my memories, and we agreed the new year would see our marriage. On that day, I'd gain my freedom, and stand beside Eldberg as his equal. I mourned still, but I wanted to believe Eldberg had changed—that he could look to what lay ahead rather than behind.

111

As the season of *Jul* began, the longhouse welcomed all. I thought back to the year now passed; of how we'd decorated Svolvaen's hall. Helka had balanced upon Eirik's shoulders, fastening the festive boughs under which our people had made merry. It was another lifetime.

In Skálavík, too, we gathered mistletoe and wreaths of green, swathing the rafters, and it became a place of merriment and games, feasting and drinking. All took their part, and there was pleasure in working side by side to fill the platters every one of us would enjoy. Many were reluctant, at first, to accept me as anything other than what I'd been, but they saw the status Eldberg afforded me and thought it wise, I supposed, to show friendlier faces. I would soon be their jarl's wife; sharing in Sigrid's bitterness would bring them no favors.

Ivar had taken to recounting a different story of the gods each day —of Loki's mischief, and Odin's cunning. He was a fine skald, assembling many about him as he assumed each voice, using gesture and song to illustrate his tales. It mattered not that the stories were already familiar. The time passed quickly.

He was beginning the tale of the Wild Hunt, telling of the army of the dead riding through the night, headed in their chase by mighty Sleipnir, Odin's eight-legged steed.

From across the room, where I helped Ragerta in seasoning joints of meat, I caught Eldberg's gaze. He'd been talking to Rangvald but gave me his slow smile. I knew well that look—that he wished to return me to his bed and make our own entertainment.

He rose and entered our chamber.

Wiping my hands, I made to join him, but had taken no more than a few steps when I saw that Rangvald followed our jarl.

'Twas a strange thing, for Eldberg rarely summoned his men for private meetings. Curiosity stirred within me, and I wondered if they planned together for the coming rituals of *Jólablót*, when our marriage was to be celebrated.

Joining the outer edges of those who listened to Ivar's story, I placed myself near the divide of our jarl's chamber from the main hall.

I could barely make out their words, for they spoke low. But with my finger pressed to one ear and the other directed toward the curtain, I discerned some of their conversation.

I heard mention of Ivar's name—that he'd been sent somewhere and recently returned, travelling as a skald.

I frowned at that. It didn't make sense. Ivar worked as a carpenter and had a family in Skálavík. He was one of Eldberg's men. Regardless of his cleverness with words, why would he wish to roam other settlements?

Rangvald spoke: Ivar had disguised himself, hunched and cloaked. He'd stayed only one night; it had been sufficient to learn what they needed.

What was this?

The next words I heard brought an icy fist to my chest.

Svolvaen.

Ivar had been to Svolvaen?

I leaned forward. What had Ivar been doing?

"He's there." Rangvald hissed, "...with a purpose...ingratiate himself with lies."

Eldberg swore. "They have allies?"

"The sister married a Bjorgen man."

Helka! They must mean Helka.

Was she alive?

"We'll be ready. None can approach unseen... double the guards on the river and the harbor... alert the watch on the headland."

They thought Svolvaen would attack? Impossible! Helka would never be so foolhardy—unless she was ignorant of Skálavík's strength.

Rangvald again. "The jarl..."

His voice dropped low. I couldn't hear.

What of the jarl?

Eirik was dead. Some other had taken his place. Olaf perhaps? Had he survived? Or Anders?

"Woken up... long time..."

Woken?

Eldberg spoke. "...come to his own slaughter... Bloodeagle..."

I clenched my nails into my palms.

Helka had told me of the bloodeagle—that Gunnolf had once inflicted it upon someone who'd refused to acknowledge him as jarl.

The man had been restrained face down, before having wings cut into his back. His ribs had then been hacked from his spine with an axe, one by one.

I sickened at the thought of it.

And there was worse. For the bones and skin on both sides had been pulled outward, followed by his lungs. Spread out like wings, Helka said, fluttering as he gasped his last breath.

No man deserved such a death.

"...blood must satisfy blood."

"Aye, my Jarl."

Feet approached the curtain. Rangvald's voice was clear. "This Eirik shall pay Svolvaen's debt."

I clutched at the curtain to prevent myself from falling.

It could not be!

Eirik—alive?

18

ELSWYTH

December 1ˢᵗ, 960AD

For so many months I'd thought Eirik dead. I'd grieved, had spent my anger and had, at last, accepted. I'd believed him gone, and I'd bargained myself to Eldberg—to save myself and my unborn child.

Could I allow myself to believe Eirik alive? Suppose Ivar were mistaken.

If my husband lived, then who else had survived that night of flames and ruin?

Would they come for me, as Eldberg seemed to think, or would they believe I'd gone willingly—a traitor to my people? There were some in Svolvaen who'd never trusted me. Would they poison Eirik's ear?

He'd forgiven me for having taken Gunnolf as my lover. He'd understood I'd thought myself forsaken. How little faith I'd had, but Eirik had borne no malice. He'd blamed himself. It was I who'd doubted; never him. Even on our wedding day, I'd kept my secrets— had failed to share my fear that the child I carried was his brother's.

And now? If we were reunited, could he accept what I'd become here in Skálavík? Could he pardon this betrayal and forgive?

If we found each other again, I vowed I'd hold nothing back. Only that, surely, would earn his trust. Only then could we be reconciled as man and wife.

And Eldberg?

I raged, and I hated him.

But I loved him, too. Something connected us. When I looked into his eyes, I recognized his pain.

What of his feelings for me?

He'd professed love, but was it real—or was I still a possession; a symbol of his victory over those who would destroy him?

There would be no use in begging him to abandon his thirst for revenge. I'd told him many times that Gunnolf—of unsound mind—must have sent the man responsible for Bretta's death; that Eirik sought only peace, and Svolvaen had instigated no aggression.

At least, that had been true before. If Eirik lived, as Ivar reported, and came for me, what then? Skálavík's warriors would be watchful. They held the advantage. Even with Bjorgen men behind him, could Eirik hope to subdue Skálavík?

I feared he'd be walking into a trap.

Somehow, I had to warn him and all Svolvaen. If I could but find my way back, how much bloodshed would be avoided—for Svolvaen and Skálavík.

To wait was torture, but I knew that my only hope of slipping away would come while Eldberg slept. I'd dress as warmly as I could—a woolen gown over both my underdresses, my cloak from fox furs Eldberg had lately given me, and foot and leg coverings I'd sewn from the same.

Through the evening, I oft refilled Eldberg's cup, needing to be certain that he wouldn't wake when I rose. His trencher I kept laden. With belly full of mead and victuals, he'd sleep most deeply.

He gave no indication of what he'd spoken of with Rangvald. Had I not overheard, I would have been none the wiser.

"Come, Elswyth, kiss me." He drew me onto his lap and cared not who witnessed his embraces.

Sigrid did not scowl as she once had used to do. Tonight, she wore a fur caplet over her gown. It occurred to me that she'd never married, running first her brother's household and now Eldberg's. Had she never wanted a man of her own? A family?

She'd had the care of Bretta, of course.

Eldberg whispered endearments to my ear. "Not long until the gods bless our wedlock, and I shall call you not just the woman I love but wife." Though I was large in the belly, his arms still reached about me. He locked his fingers at the indentation of my waist and nuzzled his mouth to my neck.

"The rest shall be forgotten. There shall be only our pledge, forsaking all others."

Had I not known all I did, I'd have thought him merely amorous, but I heard the double-edge of his words, for he believed Eirik alive, without intention of telling me. He would marry me without offering me the knowledge that would bring choice.

Despite his fine words, I was a prisoner still, for I wouldn't be permitted to return to Svolvaen. There would be no question of that.

"Aye, my lord." I touched the newly healing scars around his left eye, and those covering his cheek. "And both of us shall forgive—for naught good comes from twisting wounds, nor can love grow when we harbor deceit."

His lips twitched, but he said nothing, merely bringing my palm to his lips.

It pained me to offer a lie, but it was no less than he deserved, and I tried not to think of the betrayal Eldberg would feel when he discovered me gone.

If Eirik came to Skálavík, Eldberg would finish what he'd begun and kill the man I loved. That I would not allow; not while I had strength to prevent it.

As the hour grew late and our guests' heads nodded on their chests, I rose to speak to Thirka. Now Thoryn's wife, she looked radiant, though she'd sat shyly beside him through the feasting. Having served in the longhouse so many years, it must seem strange to be there other than as a thrall. I wondered if her mind travelled to the night upon which the fire had leapt around her and had nearly cost her everything.

"You're happy, Thirka?" I squeezed her hand. "Thoryn is a considerate husband, and the healing continues well?"

"Oh yes. With much thanks to you." She smiled. "I never thought to be so happy."

"It brings me pleasure to hear it." I drew her farther from the table, while nodding to those who sat on either side.

"You wish the same contentment for me, I think." I kept hold of her, ensuring she stood close.

"Of course." She looked uncertain. "And you are so, I hope, now that the jarl is to marry you. 'Twas not easy, but..." Her voice trailed away.

"You would help me, if there was some small thing I asked?" I lowered my voice, for none other could hear what I wished to tell her.

"In whatever way I can." She returned the pressure of my fingers.

My heart warmed. I'd no desire to imperil her, for even Thoryn would be unable to prevent Eldberg punishing Thirka if the jarl thought her complicit in my escape. But she would say whatever I asked, and willingly.

"Before I pledge myself to our jarl, there's a cleansing ritual I want to perform. I need to go alone and wash my feet in the river."

Thirka looked anxious. "But it's so very cold." She glanced down at my rounded belly. "And—"

"There's nothing to worry about." I tried to sound reassuring. "It's the way we did things in Holtholm—where I lived before. It's very... refreshing! And I'm hot all the time, with the baby growing. I'll wrap warmly—and it's just my feet. I'll be in and out swiftly."

"You want me to go with you?" Thirka asked.

"You're very kind." I sighed. "But the ritual has to be conducted alone—and there are other elements to it." I made up the details quickly. The plan wouldn't work at all if Thirka wanted to accompany me.

"There are words to be said, and I'll be addressing my old god, as well as those we all revere here in Skálavík."

"Oh!" Thirka was taken aback, suddenly uncomfortable. "And what does the jarl say?"

"It's for this that I need your help." I looked about. No one seemed to be paying attention to us. "He's very protective, and with the frost so hard, he won't want me to go."

"He'll try to stop you."

"Exactly." I inclined my head. "Carrying out the ritual is important to me, so I'm going to leave the longhouse early in morning and make my way to the river. When Eldberg wakes, he'll wonder where I am."

"You want me to tell him where you've gone?" Thirka chewed at her lip. Undoubtedly, the thought of saying anything to the jarl filled her with apprehension.

"Yes. Tell him, Thirka—just as I've explained to you. Let him know that I wouldn't let you come with me. Tell him I didn't want him to worry." I swallowed, hating myself for what I was about to say. "That I'll return later, when the ritual is complete."

It would give me more time before Eldberg came looking for me. When he did, I'd be well on my way.

19

ELSWYTH

December 2nd, 960AD

The longhouse was warm, and few wished to venture outside. At last, our guests fell asleep, lying upon the benches. Eldberg swept me to our bed with amorous intention but had drunk too much to be capable; I'd seen to that. He slept soundly, his snores as loud as any in the hall. The fire had died to glowing embers.

I cracked open the door, listening for the guards.

The moon shifted between passing clouds and the ground glowed white, reflecting what light there was. It wasn't long before I heard voices and stamping feet. They were complaining of how cold it was. They approached, then drifted away, and I stepped outside.

I'd thought myself well-clad, wrapping my hands and head—even my face—but the rawness of the night struck me. Snow was falling, though lightly. I'd have to keep moving.

I made for the forest's edge. There, I'd be hidden from view. If I kept to the shadow of the trees, I could make my way down the slope of the hill. From there, I'd use the river as my guide, but not along its banks. Instead, I'd climb upward to where the forest hugged the crags, keeping the water in sight.

At some point, I'd need to descend, to follow the river again, but that would be another day's walk. How long would it take to reach Svolvaen? By boat, the journey had taken most of the night and the morning hours. On foot, I guessed three days.

Eldberg would seek me out, I'd little doubt, but he'd be some hours behind, and there would be no tracks. The falling snow would see to that.

I'd promised not to flee, but what did such a promise mean between my enemy and myself? Hearing Eldberg speak so full of hatred still, his intent for vengeance remorseless, how could I remain?

I just needed to keep walking. All would be simple—as long as I avoided falling into the chasm, or freezing to death, or running into wolves.

Even if I were torn to pieces by some creature filled with winter hunger and met my end tonight, I would know that I'd tried. For too long I'd accepted my fate, thinking that Eirik was dead. Now, I had a reason to attempt the path back to Svolvaen.

Concealed within the trees, I reached the water, then headed upward, through the forested slopes. Keeping the sound of the river to my left, I pushed on, my cloak wrapped tight to avoid the snagging brambles.

In autumn, the forest had been full of sound. Now, it was snow-deadened. There was only the faint sound of the wind moving above, through creaking branches, and the distant rush of the river, travelling through the chasm below. The canopy gave some protection, but the flakes still fell, coming to rest on my eyelashes and nose.

One step and then another, I told myself—each footfall a soft crunch.

Drawing down the wrap from my face, I focused on my breathing —in, then out. I watched the plume of white leave my mouth.

I kept moving but stopped seeing my feet, stopped listening. Tripping over a tree root, I sank to my knees, hands planted in white. Jolted to awareness, I realized that I couldn't hear water anymore. I'd let myself wander blindly. And for how long?

121

It was too early for the sky to lighten; it would do so for only a short time in the middle of the day. How then, would I know in which direction to walk? I might only take myself farther into the forest.

I'd rest for a little while—just to regain strength. As soon as the sky lightened, wouldn't I be able to see more clearly where the trees gave way to the chasm?

I drew out the skin of water I'd thrust into my deepest pocket and touched it to my lips. I wanted to gulp at it greedily, but the liquid was too cold against my teeth.

I had some bread. Not much, but enough. I tore off a piece and held it on my tongue, softening it. There was cheese, too—the chunk half the size of my palm. Biting into it, I closed my eyes, savoring its tang.

With my cloak under me and the cloth wound close to my face, I crouched against a fallen trunk. Brushing off the snow to reveal moss, I made a crook of my elbow in which to place my head.

I hadn't intended to sleep but woke to the low call of some bird. An owl on its last nocturnal hunt? The sky was lightening, and I'd been right; to one side, the trees appeared denser, the shadows far darker. To the other, they seemed to thin, revealing daylight. The chasm had to be that way.

There was no time to lose, but the frost had entered my bones. With great effort, I unbent my knees, pushing up from the log. The pain of standing made me gasp, and I cursed myself for having lain still so long. Had I slept longer, perhaps I wouldn't have woken at all.

Which heart would have stopped first? Mine, or that of the babe inside me, nestled unknowing in warm flesh?

With faltering steps, I shuffled forward, knowing that I must keep moving—must stir my blood to warm me and make my limbs useful again.

I imagined Eldberg swinging into the saddle and setting off at a gallop. He'd sweep for signs of my trail, bending low with piercing eyes. I glanced back, half expecting to see him, but I was alone still.

Think only of what you must do.

Soon, I heard the rush of water again, growing louder as I approached. Reaching the edge of the trees, I grasped a branch and looked down. There it was—the river, and the sunlight, and a sky clear of clouds.

My progress was slow but feeling was returning to my limbs. I struggled on and, before long, the ground shelved downward. The sheer walls of the chasm were retreating, giving way to softer contours, the forest sloping to meet the water's edge.

I might have remained within the trees but wanted to feel the sun's warmth—what little of it there was. I'd descend to walk as close to the river as I could. Continuing upstream, there'd be no chance of becoming lost.

Carefully, I proceeded, keeping hold—one branch to the next. It had become much steeper and slippery, the frosted depth of powdered snow and leaves parting as my weight came down. Suddenly, I was sliding. Scooting on my behind, I skidded toward the brink, where the bank dropped away to the water. Fearful, I spread my arms, digging in my heels, needing to grasp something to stop my tumbling. Shooting past ferns and bracken, my cloak whipped from under me and my skirts rode up. I was grabbing handfuls of nothing, and the river was rushing closer.

Then, there was a jerk, and I shrieked, pulled suddenly to a halt. My cloak had caught on a stump, leaving me dangling.

I lay there for a moment, wanting to cry and laugh. I was winded and bruised and I'd scraped my hands, but I was unharmed. I just needed to gather myself. Lying here, I'd only become cold. I needed to sit up, to untangle my cloak.

The river was very close, the water rushing below my feet. I'd be able to walk here safely enough. I might even slither down and make my way directly along the river. There were stones and shingle on either side, along some stretches beside the shallows.

Rolling onto my side, I looked back up the slope. I'd been lucky not to hurt myself.

I twisted, propping myself on my elbows, and the cloak pulled taut, straining at my neck. I fumbled at the brooches pinned on either side and the strap of leather between them. But, as the thong pulled free, I was suddenly falling, staring back at my cloak, still hooked on the fallen trunk. I was clawing at fistfuls of snow and rotted matter, and then there was nothing beneath me at all.

As I hit the water, a thousand icy needles pierced me.

Gasping, I came to the surface, splashing in fright, my feet scrabbling for purchase on the riverbed. It seemed my lungs would burst, so cold was the water and the air. It seemed to freeze as it entered my body.

The rushing, icy torrent robbed me of movement, of thought. It robbed me of breath.

I'd landed just beyond the shallows, the water no deeper than my chest. However, the current was strong, sweeping back the way I'd come. With the rocks slick beneath, I fought to stand upright.

Got. To. Get. Out!

I had to push, to swim, but my limbs were already numb.

In warmer water, without my heavy skirt, I might have managed, but my gown dragged heavy. Slipping sideways, I went under again, pulled along, tumbling in the churning water until I struck against a boulder on the river's bend and emerged choking.

I clung, spreading my arms. Grasping the rock to my chest, I coughed up the water I'd swallowed. I began to sob at my foolishness, for now I would die—too weak to escape the river.

If I let go, all would be over. The babe I carried would never draw breath. I'd never see Eirik again. I was afraid to do so—to be swept from this life.

And then, above the rushing around my ears, I heard the whinny of a horse and a man's voice, stern in command. A stallion was upon me, kicking up spray from the shallows. Its rider was swathed in coarse fur. The face that looked down was filled with fury, barely contained.

Guiding the horse into the deeper trench, Eldberg leaned over to wrench me upward, clasping me under the arms to sit before him in the saddle.

Without uttering a word, he turned us back to the shallows and urged the stallion into a canter. Shivering, I laid my head to his chest. I had nothing left, and my tears fell silently as water streamed from my sodden clothes and hair.

It was over.

Eldberg

Since before first light, he'd ridden upstream, looking for signs of her passing, for where she was perhaps hiding, or where she might have left the river. There were crevices all along the chasm which could be climbed, leading into the forest.

Thirka had come to him, Thoryn at her side, to explain Elswyth's absence, and had seemed to believe what she'd told him—that Elswyth had risen early to perform a cleansing ritual. But he'd been suspicious at once. A blizzard had blown through during the night, and she was close enough to her time of delivering the child to make such an outing foolhardy.

If she'd heard Rangvald or Ivar talking, or what had passed between himself and Rangvald, it would be reason enough for her to make for Svolvaen.

Still, to find her gone had enraged him. She'd come to him as a captive, and he'd used her with little mercy in those first days, but hadn't he shown her how his feelings had changed? Hadn't he showered her with gifts and made her life one of ease? More than that. He'd bestowed the highest honor in asking her to be his wife. She'd thrown everything back in his face. She'd forsaken him.

Now, he carried her, wet to the bone and shivering, into the bathhouse. He'd left instruction with Ragerta to stoke the fire and fill the barrel deep. Swiftly, he pulled off Elswyth's sodden clothing, then his own.

She offered no resistance as he lowered her in, limp in his arms. Beneath the water, he attempted to rub life back into her body. Her teeth continued to chatter, but she looked at him, touching his chest.

There was much in her expression, though she said nothing as he kneaded the length of her limbs, her hands and fingers, feet and toes. Her lips were tinged blue. He saw again the resemblance—those eyes looking up at him...so very like...

Dipping her, he let the water cover the back of her head. When he raised her again, he noticed blood trickling—a gash which the warmth had opened up. Turning her head, he looked behind her ear, where he'd so often kissed, just above the little mole. Lifting her hair, he saw the wound; it seemed small enough not to need sewing.

He parted the hair on either side, checking that he hadn't missed anything more.

Beneath his fingers, he felt them before he saw them. Two more moles. With the one just below her hairline, they formed the familiar shape.

His fingers trembled.

How had he missed this?

How had he not seen?

So many times, the likeness had struck him, but he'd pushed it from his mind. Now, he understood.

It was the same mark worn by all of Beornwold's line: a triangle behind the ear. Beornwold's had been dark and prominent. Sigrid's moles were fainter. Bretta's had been the same as those on Elswyth's skin, barely raised. Elswyth's hairline had covered the other moles, but they'd been there all the time.

And those eyes—so like Bretta's.

Who was she?

20

ELSWYTH

December 3ʳᵈ, 960AD

E ldberg held my face in his hands.

I'd expected him to berate me; at the very least, to scold me for foolishness. But his initial anger had dissipated, replaced by intensity of a different sort—as if he perceived something he'd been unaware of before, and were seeing me for the first time.

There was hesitation in his growling voice. "Elswyth, I must know…"

Just then, the door flung wide.

Thoryn stood on the threshold. From beyond, there was shouting and a rush of movement. "A raid, my Jarl!" Thoryn was breathless. "They were spotted on the uppermost cliffs, where the forest meets the mountain. The headland guard has been struck down! I've commanded men to remain at the harbor and along the river, in case this is a diversion, but we're rallying all to arms to meet the attackers."

Eldberg rose from the water, dragging on his clothes. Though his axe and short dagger hung from his belt, he was without longer blade.

"Give me your sword."

"My Jarl?" I'd never seen Thoryn falter in obeying Eldberg, but a man's sword was an extension of his arm. With reluctance, he unsheathed it. Thoryn's had the *Valknut* carved into the hilt: Odin's symbol—three interlocking triangles with the power of life over death.

"Stay here, Thoryn. Protect her. Hide her in the forest if necessary —but she's not to be taken."

Eldberg flung one last look upon me and was gone.

Thoryn stood frowning, evidently displeased. Casting about, he saw first my wet clothes upon the floor and then another gown, dry and clean, folded to one side. Ragerta must have left it for me.

He threw the towel. "Be swift, Elswyth. I'll guard the door while you dress."

I felt as if I could lay down and sleep for a whole day and night, but I worked as quickly as I was able. My fingers tingled strangely, still partly numb, and my hands shook as I laced my bootlets; they were damp from the river, but I needed to be ready. At any moment, Thoryn might insist on moving position, and I'd no wish to go bare-foot through the snow.

Outside, the shouts grew louder. I recognized the ring of blade hitting blade. Was it as Rangvald had warned—that the survivors of Svolvaen had called their Bjorgen allies to aid them? And for what purpose had they come? If Eirik were alive, as Ivar had said, was he here? I could scarcely let myself believe it, and yet I hoped.

Thoryn drew out the shiv from his belt. "Take it, and be prepared to use it."

I'd only used a knife to prepare meat, never to kill anyone. And why would I now? The men of Svolvaen would know me and would never harm me.

But what of Bjorgen's warriors? They, you've never met.

I touched its slender spike.

"Under the ribs, here." Thoryn pointed. "Push hard, and it'll go straight through. Or behind if you need to—just the same, into the soft organs."

He clasped his axe. "I must see how the fight goes." He nodded to me before easing up the latch. Bringing his face close, he peered out through the opening but, in the same instant, the door flung back.

A figure leapt into the room, silhouetted against the fading light. His shield blocked Thoryn's blade. The two wrangled, their axes locking as they pushed against one another. Then, Thoryn shouted in surprise. He fell back, lowering his axe.

"Sweyn!"

"Aye, 'tis me!" He kicked the door shut.

I'd shrunk to the far wall, the shiv's handle tight in my palm, its steel cool, flattened against the underside of my wrist.

"Just what I've been looking for."

Thoryn, uncertain, looked from Sweyn to me and back again. "You disappeared without a word. Why, brother? Were we not worthy enough—the men who've stood by your side since we first held our wooden swords? You wished so badly to leave us?"

Sweyn narrowed his eyes. "You ask me that? Where was your loyalty when Beornwold died? I was his favorite until Eldberg came. He would have chosen me to take his place; chosen me to marry Bretta. I was our jarl's second before that berserker scum gained the old man's trust, but none in Skálavík spoke for my claim. Where was your brotherhood then? Or was that your own jealousy? You'd rather see a stranger rule than bow to me?"

Thoryn shook his head. "So much anger, *bróðir*. Don't the gods show us the folly of kin turning on kin?"

"And this one." Sweyn jerked his head in my direction. "She's no kin at all, but that matters not. Eldberg knows no loyalty, and nor does she—a whore who makes her bed where it's softest."

A dawning awareness seemed to come to Thoryn. "You were looking for her? Did you not think her dead, Sweyn—since you left her so?"

"I had to be sure." He curled his lip. "Before I slit the throat of the last man of the headland watch, I found out what I needed to know—that the bitch yet lived."

Thoryn held his axe aloft again, but his face was full of sorrow. "You betrayed us."

"Aye! And 'twas easy! Those Svolvaen fools believed readily enough that I'd tried to help their precious Elswyth." His face contorted in a mocking sneer. "So sad that we were separated in the forest!"

Sweyn tossed aside his shield, placing both hands on his axe.

"I'd thought only to find shelter there, but they're stronger than we realized with their Bjorgen friends. There's enough of them to take Skálavík— and it's I who'll be given command when they do."

Thoryn was nimble, swinging his axe towards Sweyn's chest, but Sweyn was speedier, arresting the blow and sending his own blade into Thoryn's upper arm.

I cried out as Thoryn crumpled. He slumped to the floor, groaning and clutching the wound.

Sweyn gazed down at him. "'Twas my bargain, to lead them here, bringing them up through the chasm in the cliffs. You remember how we discovered the crevice, and the pact we made to keep all secret? Our special place, that no other knew of."

Pulling his arm into his chest, Thoryn winced. "You're some changeling, sent to destroy what we've built."

Sweyn pushed him lightly with his foot. "If you be right, then I truly owe Skálavík nothing and shall take from it what I see fit."

Tipping back his head, Thoryn grimaced. "And you helped our enemy all along, I suppose, with that worm who set the longhouse blazing."

"Oh no! That you have quite wrong." Sweyn's laughter was mirthless. "I found the sorry cur spying on us, right enough, on the edge of the forest, but it was I who shot those arrows. A rewarding hunting trip, indeed, for I caught a scapegoat for my misdeed, and broke his jaw before dragging him to our jarl."

Hearing those words, the room swam before me. All this time, Eldberg had believed Gunnolf's man responsible for the fire that killed his wife. On this basis, he'd attacked Svolvaen and blamed Eirik equally with his brother. But Sweyn had been the viper, waiting to send his venom to Skálavík's heart.

Thoryn closed his eyes. "And what now, Sweyn? You must kill me, for I'll not permit your foul villainy—not while I live."

"Aye, you'll die, and the whore with you. Look how she quivers." His voice dripped with contempt. "There shall be none alive to contradict my story."

As Sweyn bent to Thoryn, placing his hands about his neck, I flung myself across the room, to plunge the shiv with all my might deep into Sweyn's side.

He screamed in agony—in rage. Twisting, he tried to pluck it out, but I leapt forward again, jerking the blade free. He lurched to one side, disbelieving as the blood spurted from the wound.

I glanced at Thoryn. He was pale, but his lips moved, urging me to act.

On his knees, Sweyn was groping for the axe he'd let drop. Steeling myself, I jumped upon him and drove the shiv home again, clear through his neck.

With a cry of horror, I recoiled, watching as Sweyn fell. This time, there was no scream—only the gurgle of a man trying desperately to breathe. He struggled briefly before his head fell back, and he moved no more.

"Elswyth." Thoryn's voice rasped. "Help me!"

His tunic was stained crimson. He was weak, but conscious still. Where the blade had entered, the fabric was ripped and I tore it farther, to better see the wound. It was deep and the blood rising dark.

Grabbing the towels, I wadded one, pressing it to the open flesh. I bid Thoryn hold it while I brought the other cloth around, binding all tight. Pulling Thoryn, I brought him more securely into the corner. Even if he fainted, he would remain upright. It would give him more time. Though, if he lived, it would be the gods' will, for I could do nothing more without needle and thread.

To find those, I'd need to leave where we were.

I'd need to reach the longhouse.

21

ELSWYTH

December 3rd, 960AD

Since Sweyn had entered, I'd paid no heed to the commotion outside. Now, I heard the clash of metal and the screams of men —not immediately outside but farther down the hill. I was fearful to confront what lay beyond the door, but I needed to help Thoryn, and myself.

I wiped the shiv clean on Sweyn's tunic and took a deep breath.

The cold was cruel after the warmth of the bathhouse, and I'd no cloak for my shoulders, but there was no time to think of comfort—only of action.

Wounded men, the dead and dying, lay between me and the long-house. However, there were none to prevent me reaching it. Seeing me, some called out, and my heart was torn as I hurried past.

The snow, falling gently, was already covering the bodies, while that beneath them was stained scarlet.

In twenty paces, I reached the great hall and paused for breath, leaning my head against the open doorway. From inside came the sound of furniture being pushed aside.

Someone was there.

A Bjorgen warrior, greedy for spoils while his brothers fought? Or a Svolvaen man, who could lead me to Eirik?

Holding the shiv before me, I darted within, pressing my back to the wall.

A voice came from the far chamber—Sigrid's.

"Take what you like. I won't stop you!" She was frightened, discovered in her hiding place. There was a clatter of something overturned, then a shriek. "Don't hurt me, please!"

I cursed. For all that I disliked Sigrid, I couldn't stand by and allow her to be harmed. Swiftly, I made my way across the space. Beneath Sigrid's loom were several sacks of wool, yet to be spun, and I caught one with my foot. There was a squeak, then a low mumble. Two pairs of eyes peeped out.

Ragerta and Thirka!

Seeing me, they crept out, grasping my hands, drawing me into their embrace. They were as pleased to see me as I them, but there was no time to waste. With my finger pressed to my lips, I pointed toward the cooking knives.

"I don't know anything!" Sigrid screeched from beyond the curtain.

Wielding our weapons, we yanked aside the cloth.

On the floor, her assailant was twisting Sigrid's arm behind her back. The torturer looked up and, seeing me, gave a snort of surprise.

"Helka!" I dropped the shiv and rushed to her.

The next moment, Leif appeared, locking Thirka and Ragerta about the neck.

"'Tis all right." I motioned the women to lower their blades. "We're friends here."

"We've come for you, Elswyth, to bring you home." Helka stood tall, her eyes glinting fire. "And to avenge those who died in Svolvaen. We'll make Skálavík pay!"

"No!" I couldn't bear it. This fighting must cease before more lost their lives. "Skálavík was betrayed!"

Taking Sigrid's hand, I pulled her up. "It was Sweyn. He's deceived everyone. He set the fire that killed Bretta!"

Sigrid's hand flew to her mouth and her face crumpled. "I don't believe it! You're up to your cunning tricks again!"

I could have shaken her for such stupidity. "Thoryn knows. He heard Sweyn confess."

Thoryn!

I turned to Thirka, telling her to go to the bathhouse and take everything necessary. Ragerta would help. If they could stop the bleeding, he had a chance.

"This Sweyn, who led us here"—Helka made me look at her—"He said naught of this; only of his grievances, and that he tried to help you."

White hot fury surged through my veins. "He wanted to kill me. He's without honor or truth, serving only himself. All this—" I found, suddenly, that I was crying. "Everything. It's his work."

"Come, Leif, we'll tear each limb from his body and fling him from the cliffs!" Picking up her weapons, Helka pushed past Sigrid.

"He's dead already." I held up the shiv. "By my hand."

Helka stopped immediately. Turning, she stood for a moment, only looking at me. Then, her gaze dropped to my belly. She clasped me to her again.

"Always fighting for your life, brave one." She buried her face in my hair.

"Eirik?" I had to know. "He's alive? He's here?" My heart pounded.

Eldberg was possessed by hatred that would accept no outcome other than Eirik's death. If he found him, he would kill him—even if it brought his own end.

I could not deny that I loved them both, though in different ways.

To think of either being hurt or dying!

I couldn't bear it.

Helka nodded. "We'll find a way to stop this madness." Unstrapping the crossbow from her back, she passed it to me. "You remember how to use this?"

Eirik

Eirik gripped his sword—the weapon that had served him through all time, his Heart of the Slain. Raising his prayer to Thor and Odin, he asked for their strength.

Running to meet the advancing foe, Eirik sent his blade into a man's stomach. His axe sliced through another's neck. Amidst skewered flesh and splitting skulls, he was aware of his warrior brethren and the Bjorgen warriors fighting alongside.

But, his purpose was single-minded.

Eldberg!

Who'd brought vengeance to Svolvaen for a crime laid only at Gunnolf's door.

Who'd killed men and women innocent of misdeed.

Who'd kidnapped his wife, degrading her as his bed-thrall!

He'd heard of the cruelties of his adversary, and the brute strength which brought annihilation to his enemies.

If Elswyth were alive, only this man's death would free her.

Across the fray, Eirik saw him: taller by far than anyone else, his head without helmet, his hair a wild mass of copper, and his face scarred upon the left side.

The throng of battle seemed to part as Eirik gazed upon Skálavík's jarl.

"Time to taste my blade, Eldberg!"

Those about them fell back, making way for the two whose encounter would shape all that was to come. Through the fading light, each took measure of his foe.

"Or have you bravery only for skulking in the night, abducting women—like Beornwold before you."

In reply, Eldberg thundered forward. He bore down with a fearful war cry. His first strike might have felled Eirik before he'd offered a single blow, but Eirik threw himself to one side, rolling away. Leaping up, he raised his shield to ward off the next. It was swift in coming. Eldberg's sword rang from the metal edge.

Eirik kept his feet firm but managed not a single thrust in retaliation, barely defending himself against the attack Eldberg rained down upon him. He was tiring, straining to withstand the onslaught.

Helka had warned him; his strength was not as it had been.

Despite the freezing air, sweat drenched his body. He needed only one sure hit—a quick motion, stabbing under Eldberg's raised arm, into unprotected flesh.

As Eldberg's weapon fell again, Eirik levelled his sword. Now was the time to strike, between his enemy's blows.

However, Eldberg seemed to anticipate his move. With a groan, Eirik blocked the weight of plunging steel. He staggered, faltering, then dropped to one knee.

The snow's light flakes fell upon his heated skin.

In silent horror, Eirik witnessed Eldberg's sword enter his shoulder, slicing through muscle, flesh, and bone. The force broke the blade in two, leaving him impaled.

Elswyth, my love, where are you?

From far away, there was a scream.

Eldberg

Eldberg pushed Eirik flat beneath his booted foot. Drawing up his enemy's tunic, he laid his back bare. From his belt, he took his axe. He'd promised to deliver the bloodeagle, and he would have his prize. First, he'd peel back the skin, then he'd hack the ribs from the spine. As he plunged his hands in this man's blood, he'd offer the death to Odin. As to the lungs, he'd burn them and let the smoke carry to Valhalla as proof of his victory.

Standing, he raised his axe high above his head and bellowed his triumph.

Many of those who'd been fighting had fallen back, seeing Svolvaen's jarl at the mercy of the Beast.

Eldberg looked about him, reveling in his conquest.

Let all behold and fear!

None would take what was his.

Skálavík!
Elswyth!
And his true revenge!
He would be denied nothing.

Elswyth

Helka would never reach them in time. I had to shoot and pray that my aim was true.

Only as the arrow pierced his shoulder did Eldberg see me. The axe dropped from his grip, and his face turned full to mine. It showed first disbelief, then agonized sorrow, as if a searing light had been extinguished.

I had betrayed him.

He staggered and pitched forward.

22

ELSWYTH

December 3rd, 960AD

I loved them both.

I didn't know how this could be, but it was true.

Eldberg refused at first to look at me, though he allowed me to clean and bind the wound. I'd made my choice clear, in taking arms against him. The injury I'd inflicted might forever pain him.

"You loved your wife. You must understand." I sat beside the bed we'd shared.

Whatever Eldberg imagined he felt for me, it was not love. He desired, I think, to see in me what he'd lost, but I would never be Bretta.

And he was not Eirik.

He wished me to love him, as he had come to yearn for me, but this would never be.

Eirik was the husband I'd chosen.

"There is much you do not know." He regarded me warily, as if it was too painful or too dangerous to keep my gaze. "The gash behind your ear—"

I touched it, gingerly. It remained tender.

"You have a mole—" He paused. "There are two more, within your hair. Three altogether."

"What of it? Many have such marks on their skin."

"Not like this. Many times, I saw her in you. Wishful thinking, I believed, but there was more to it than that. Sigrid saw it, too, though she didn't want to accept."

Eldberg believed I was of Beornwold's line; that the babe I carried was Beornwold's grandchild, and that Bretta had been my half-sister.

I'd told him long ago of how I was conceived—by rape of my mother during a Viking raid. It had been more than twenty years ago, before Eldberg joined Beornwold's service.

I'd always known that I belonged elsewhere.

After all that had happened, all that I'd endured, to find that Skálavík was that place! That my father had been here all along. And a sister...

It changed nothing between Eldberg and I, but it provided a stronger reason for Svolvaen and Skálavík to put aside their blood feud. The clans had been joined, years ago, through Ingrid of Skálavík, Eirik's grandmother.

Now, the child I carried would join the two again.

I told Eldberg of what Sweyn had boasted. He was responsible for the fire, his ambition being stronger than loyalty.

Gunnolf, half-mad as he'd been, had not planned the attack.

Thoryn gave testament, having heard every foul confession from Sweyn's lips. Eldberg nodded in acceptance. It was as if he'd always known the truth of it. He'd retaliated against Svolvaen when no blame lay among its people.

"You'll speak with Eirik and agree a truce. For my sake, for whatever love you bear me, you'll set aside the past."

Eldberg nodded wearily. "Not just for your sake, but for Bretta's. 'Tis fitting that you killed he who took her life. I shall never forget, nor forgive, but 'tis a door I must close, or I shall lose my reason—and my will to remain in this world."

I brought his hand to my cheek.

There was good in him; that I believed with all my heart.

139

Many had been injured, and many killed. The longhouse was filled with men needing treatment. Sigrid helped, with Ragerta and Thirka, though she would not speak to me.

She'd shown me nothing but ill-will, viewing me as an interloper. When Eldberg told her what he knew, perhaps her manner would soften. Meanwhile, I was content with friendship borne of true kindness, which those of gentlest heart offered freely.

Gradually, Thoryn regained his strength, and Eldberg, too; though neither would wield a weapon as they once had—at least not with their left arms.

It was Eirik's bedside I kept through the coming weeks—Eldberg having granted haven to all Svolvaen's wounded. He'd come too soon to battle and had barely strength to endure this fresh wound, but I believed he would recover. My indomitable Eirik!

A signal had been cast from the clifftops soon after the battle, calling the waiting ships into the fjord. Leif and Helka sailed without delay, with those fit to take oars, returning them to Svolvaen and Bjorgen.

Our treaty was struck—for Skálavík to retain its independence, though the Bjorgen forces had brought those of Skálavík to their knees. Ships of both Svolvaen and Bjorgen would be welcomed in the harbor and given preference in all terms of trade. In times of need, we pledged each to come to the others' aid.

I told Eirik of my capture and the bargain I'd made with Eldberg to keep myself alive. In the name of the peace that must be, for the good of Svolvaen, he accepted what was done, though I saw it ate at his heart.

As to the babe growing within me, once his wonder had passed, I saw the uncertainty that burdened him.

"There is something between you and Eldberg?" he asked. "You must tell me, Elswyth. If there is love—" His face contorted, for he could not speak all his fears. "And this child…"

"Nay, husband." I brought my lips to his, letting him feel my love through my kiss. "Only you have my heart, and the babe is due two moons from now."

At once, hope replaced despair, but there was more to be said. I had to tell him everything. We could not build a future on half-truths. "Almost a year ago, you went away, and much happened that brought me sorrow."

"You told me of it," Eirik replied. "Of Gunnolf's cruelty and his demands of you. Had he lived, I would have challenged him to the death for how he treated you. As it is, the gods delivered their own justice for his betrayal."

I shook my head, my eyes stinging. "But, the child—" My bravery failed me. "What if—"

Eirik spread his fingers wide over my stomach. "I will love the child, whether it bears my brother's blood or my own." He managed a weary smile. "I'll teach the boy to be a brave warrior—that he may take the mantle of Svolvaen's rule."

"And if we have a daughter?" I raised an eyebrow, pushing away my tears.

"I'll teach her just the same. She'll be like her aunt, Helka."

I pressed my hand over his, filled with new joy. Life was growing inside me. A child we'd raise together. Much had been lost: my mother and grandmother, and the boys with whom I'd grown up, my first home left behind, my lady Asta, and so many of Svolvaen.

Life was fragile, and happiness too precious to throw away. It was worth fighting for. I didn't know if we could put aside all remorse, but I knew we must try.

"You still believe me worthy of taking my place beside you, as your wife?" I was almost afraid to meet Eirik's gaze, for I knew nothing would be hidden there.

He looked truly into my eyes. "You're stronger than any woman— even than Helka! By Odin, you've the determination of ten men! It is I who must strive to prove myself worthy of you."

He buried his face against my belly. "I thank the gods you're still alive. I shall make sacrifices as soon as we are home, to beseech them that nothing shall part us while we yet walk this earth. There is no peace for me in a world without you."

We kissed then, tenderly and long, remembering the feel of each other's lips and the wonder that was our love. It would only grow stronger, for we had both learned what was real—belief and trust and belonging.

I touched the old scar that ran down Eirik's brow and cheek. There were many more, across his torso and back. Of my own, most were hidden deep inside, but they were as real as Eirik's.

Once, I might have wished them away, but I knew better now. The scars were reminders of all we'd lived through.

EPILOGUE

February 2ⁿᵈ, 961AD

I clutched Eirik's hand, bracing against the rising swell of pain.

Ragerta passed a cold cloth over my forehead. "'Twill be some time yet."

Thirka nodded as my features eased. "And the jarl, he might take some air."

Eirik looked haggard but said, "I'll not leave."

Through the night, the two women wet my lips and murmured prayers over me, but my fortitude waned. I could barely cry out against the spasms. My breathing grew shallow, like the lamp's dimming flicker.

It was near dawn when Ragerta shook my shoulder. "'Tis time. You must bear down and push the child."

"No more... Just sleep..." I wished to close my eyes again, but Eirik rubbed my hand between his own.

He looked pale. "Soon we shall have our child, and our lives will begin a new season—but you must fight!" Moving to the top of the bed, he brought my shoulders to rest upon his chest. "Together, we shall do this, wife. You have my strength and your own."

I did as he asked, forcing all my will into the child.

"The head!" Thirka shouted. "Again, Elswyth, and the babe is here!"

Eirik's arms were firm about me. Again, I strained, pushing the pain downward. I was repaid with the sensation of a great shifting—of a weight moving within me.

I gasped and fell back into Eirik's embrace.

Ragerta lifted the child for us to see, and there was a lusty cry. "'Tis perfect—a fine daughter!"

She laid the babe on my chest, and tears sprang to my eyes. Through all the sorrow, I was delivered of the child I'd longed for— the most precious treasure. She was the creation of my body, miraculous, and belonging to me as nothing else had ever done.

While she nuzzled to my breast, Eirik pressed his mouth to my ear. He whispered, "I have everything." Lifting her tiny hand, his face was full of pride.

Her hair was pale, like my own and like Eirik's.

If she was Gunnolf's, there was nothing in her appearance yet to show it. Perhaps we'd never be sure. Perhaps it would never matter.

She was mine and Eirik's—and I prayed she would know, always, what it was to be loved.

Doesn't Eldberg deserve his own 'happy ever after'?

Look out for a new series of adventures, featuring Eldberg and his most loyal men.
Each has a heroine waiting for them, well-matched to stubborn hearts.

Want to be first in the know when the new series releases?

Sign-up via Emmanuelle's website, to receive news to your inbox.
www.emmanuelledemaupassant.com

Love darkly brooding historical romance?

Emmanuelle has some new series of darker romance planned - writing under her pen name of Anna Quinn.

Sign up to receive first eyes on the deliciousness!

And check monthly, for news to your inbox.

First name

Email address

What are you interested in hearing about?

☑ dark Viking romance
☐ dark vampire romance
☑ dark romance audio books

CLICK HERE TO SUBMIT

FURTHER WORKS

BY EMMANUELLE DE MAUPASSANT

Dangerous Desire
One encounter changes everything.

When the Earl of Rancliffe suffers humiliation at the hands of the mysterious Mademoiselle Noire, he vows revenge. But his anger soon becomes obsession, as she leads him into ever more dangerous games.

As cruel as she is beautiful, Mademoiselle Noire has no intention of revealing her true identity, nor of entangling her heart.
But in a world of vice and dark desire, what does her heart secretly yearn for?

Devour this boxed set, which comprises all three darkly sensual romances from the 'Dangerous Desire' trilogy.

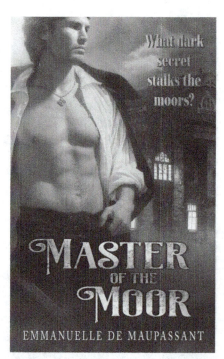

<u>Master of the Moor</u>

What happens when a brooding hero meets an unscrupulous heroine, who'll do anything to make a suitable match?

The winds howl and mist creeps over the dark cliffs of Dartmoor as the enigmatic Mallon and ravishing Geneviève meet at Wulverton Hall.

Discover Emmanuelle's 'Lady's Guide' series: historical romance brimming with mystery, passion and intrigue.

The Lady's Guide to a Highlander's Heart

The Lady's Guide to Mistletoe and Mayhem

The Lady's Guide to Escaping Cannibals

The Lady's Guide to Scandal

The Lady's Guide to Deception and Desire

The Lady's Guide to Tempting a Transylvanian Count

NINE CONQUERING REASONS TO SURRENDER

Dare to Enter our World

Battle-hardened and broad-chested, with shoulders built for carrying you to bed, these Vikings are pure muscle, and pure determination.

Delivered into Viking hands, the brides of Achnaryrie now belong to their conquering masters but, as wedding nights bring surrender to duty, will fierce lovers also surrender their hearts?

The Highland wilderness is savage, life is perilous, and the future uncertain, but each Viking has sworn protection, and there are no lengths to which a man will not go to safeguard the woman he loves.

ABOUT THE AUTHOR

Emmanuelle de Maupassant lives in the Highlands with her husband and her hairy pudding terrier, Archie, (connoisseur of squeaky toys and bacon treats).

For behind the scenes chat, you may like to join
Emmanuelle's Boudoir, on Facebook.